OU... ...iest
sati... ...t. In
the character of Tricky, self-proclaimed legal
whiz, peace-loving Quaker—and, somehow,
President of the United States—Roth has
created a hypocritical opportunist who hides
his heartlessness behind the clichés and pieties
of high office. Tricky's public language is a
merciless parody of that 'candid' Presidential
prose that is no more than double-talk.

OUR GANG is conceived in indignation, a
satirical vision of a debased national leadership
speaking a language that in Orwell's words,
is 'designed to make lies sound truthful and
murder respectable, and to give an appearance
of solidity to pure wind.'

Also by PHILIP ROTH

GOODBYE, COLUMBUS
LETTING GO
PORTNOY'S COMPLAINT

and published by CORGI BOOKS

Philip Roth

Our Gang
(Starring Tricky and His Friends)

CORGI BOOKS
A DIVISION OF TRANSWORLD PUBLISHERS LTD
A NATIONAL GENERAL COMPANY

OUR GANG (STARRING TRICKY AND HIS FRIENDS)
A CORGI BOOK 0 552 08976 1

Originally published in Great Britain
by Jonathan Cape Ltd.

PRINTING HISTORY
Jonathan Cape edition published 1971
Corgi edition published 1972

Sections of this book appeared in somewhat different
form in *Modern Occasions* and *The New York Review of Books*

This book is set in Plantin 10/11 pt.

Corgi Books are published by Transworld Publishers, Ltd.,
Cavendish House, 57–59 Uxbridge Road, Ealing,
London, W.5.

Made and printed in Great Britain by
Richard Clay (The Chaucer Press), Ltd., Bungay, Suffolk.

To MILDRED MARTIN of Bucknell University,
ROBERT MAURER now of Antioch College,
and NAPIER WILT of the University of Chicago—
three teachers to whom I remain particularly
grateful for the instruction and encouragement
they gave me

... And I remember frequent Discourses with my Master concerning the Nature of Manhood, in other Parts of the World; having Occasion to talk of *Lying*, and *false Representation*, it was with much Difficulty that he comprehended what I meant; although he had otherwise a most acute Judgement. For he argued thus; That the Use of Speech was to make us understand one another, and to receive Information of Facts; now if anyone *said the Thing which was not*, these Ends were defeated; because I cannot properly be said to understand him; and I am so far from receiving Information, that he leaves me worse than in Ignorance; for I am led to believe a Thing *Black* when it is *White*, and *Short* when it is *Long*. And these were all the Notions he had concerning that Faculty of Lying, so perfectly well understood, and so universally practised among human Creatures.

—Jonathan Swift, *A Voyage to the Houyhnhnms*, 1726

... one ought to recognize that the present political chaos is connected with the decay of language, and that one can probably bring about some improvement by starting at the verbal end. . . . Political language—and with variations this is true of all political parties, from Conservatives to Anarchists—is designed to make lies sound truthful and murder respectable, and to give an appearance of solidity to pure wind.

—George Orwell, 'Politics and the English Language,' 1946

CONTENTS

OUR GANG
(STARRING TRICKY AND HIS FRIENDS)

FROM PERSONAL AND RELIGIOUS BELIEFS I CONSIDER ABORTIONS AN UNACCEPTABLE FORM OF POPULATION CONTROL. FURTHERMORE, UNRESTRICTED ABORTION POLICIES, OR ABORTION ON DEMAND, I CANNOT SQUARE WITH MY PERSONAL BELIEF IN THE SANCTITY OF HUMAN LIFE—INCLUDING THE LIFE OF THE YET UNBORN. FOR, SURELY, THE UNBORN HAVE RIGHTS ALSO, RECOGNIZED IN LAW, RECOGNIZED EVEN IN PRINCIPLES EXPOUNDED BY THE UNITED NATIONS.

RICHARD NIXON,
SAN CLEMENTE, APRIL 3, 1971

ONE

TRICKY COMFORTS A
TROUBLED CITIZEN

CITIZEN: Sir, I want to congratulate you for coming out on April 3 for the sanctity of human life, including the life of the yet unborn. That required a lot of courage, especially in light of the November election results.

TRICKY: Well, thank you. I know I could have done the popular thing, of course, and come out *against* the sanctity of human life. But frankly I'd rather be a one-term President and do what I believe is right than be a two-term President by taking an easy position like that. After all, I have got my conscience to deal with, as well as the electorate.

CITIZEN: Your conscience, sir, is a marvel to us all.

TRICKY: Thank you.

CITIZEN: I wonder if I may ask you a question having to do with Lieutenant Calley and his conviction for killing twenty-two Vietnamese civilians at My Lai.

TRICKY: Certainly. I suppose you are bringing that up as another example of my refusal to do the popular thing.

CITIZEN: How's that, sir?

TRICKY: Well, in the wake of the public outcry against that conviction, the popular thing—the most popular thing by far—would have been for me, as Commander-in-Chief, to have convicted the twenty-two unarmed civilians of conspiracy to murder Lieutenant Calley. But if you read your papers, you'll see I refused to do that, and chose only to review the question of his guilt, and not theirs. As I said, I'd rather be a one-term President. And may I make one thing more perfectly clear, while we're on the subject of Vietnam? I am not going to interfere in the internal affairs of another country. If Presi-

11

dent Thieu has sufficient evidence and wishes to try those twenty-two My Lai villagers posthumously, according to some Vietnamese law having to do with ancestor worship, that is his business. But I assure you, I in no way intend to interfere with the workings of the Vietnamese system of justice. I think President Thieu, and the duly elected Saigon officials, can 'hack' it alone in the law and order department.

CITIZEN: Sir, the question that's been troubling me is this. Inasmuch as I share your belief in the sanctity of human life——

TRICKY: Good for you. I'll bet you're quite a football fan, too.

CITIZEN: I am, sir. Thank you, sir ... But inasmuch as I feel as you do about the unborn, I am seriously troubled by the possibility that Lieutenant Calley may have committed an abortion. I hate to say this, Mr. President, but I am seriously troubled when I think that one of those twenty-two Vietnamese civilians Lieutenant Calley killed may have been a pregnant woman.

TRICKY: Now just one minute. We have a tradition in the courts of this land that a man is innocent until he is proven guilty. There were babies in that ditch at My Lai, and we know there were women of all *ages* but I have not seen a single document that suggests the ditch at My Lai contained a *pregnant* woman.

CITIZEN: But what *if*, sir—what *if* one of the twenty-two was a pregnant woman? Suppose that were to come to light in your judicial review of the lieutenant's conviction. In that you personally believe in the sanctity of human life, including the life of the yet unborn, couldn't such a fact seriously prejudice you against Lieutenant Calley's appeal? I have to admit that as an opponent of abortion, it would have a profound effect upon me.

TRICKY: Well, it's very honest of you to admit it. But as a trained lawyer, I think I might be able to go at the matter in a somewhat less emotional manner. First off, I would have to ask whether Lieutenant Calley was *aware* of the fact that the woman in question was pregnant *before* he killed her. Clearly, if she was not yet 'showing,' I think you would in all fairness have to conclude that the lieutenant could have had no knowledge of her pregnancy, and thus, in no sense of the word, would he have committed an abortion.

CITIZEN: What if she *told* him she was pregnant?

TRICKY: Good question. She might indeed have tried to tell him. But in that Lieutenant Calley is an American who speaks only English, and the My Lai villager is a Vietnamese who speaks only Vietnamese, there could have been no possible means of verbal communication. And as for sign language, I don't believe we can hang a man for failing to understand what must surely have been the gestures of a hysterical, if not deranged, woman.

CITIZEN: No, that wouldn't be fair, would it.

TRICKY: In short then, if the woman was not 'showing,' Lieutenant Calley could *not* be said to have engaged in an unacceptable form of population control, and it would be possible for me to square what he did with my personal belief in the sanctity of human life, including the life of the yet unborn.

CITIZEN: But, sir, what if she *was* 'showing'?

TRICKY: Well then, as good lawyers we would have to ask another question. Namely: did Lieutenant Calley believe the woman to be pregnant, or did he, mistakenly, in the heat of the moment, assume that she was just stout? It's all well and good for us to be Monday Morning My Lai Quarterbacks, you know, but there's a war going on out there, and you cannot always expect an officer rounding up unarmed civilians to be able to distinguish between an ordinary fat Vietnamese woman and one who is in the middle, or even the late, stages of pregnancy. Now if the pregnant ones would wear maternity clothes, of course, that would be a great help to our boys. But in that they don't, in that all of them seem to go around all day in their pajamas, it is almost impossible to tell the men from the women, let alone the pregnant from the nonpregnant. Inevitably then—and this is just one of those unfortunate things about a war of this kind—there is going to be confusion on this whole score of who is who out there. I understand that

13

we are doing all we can to get into the hamlets with American-style maternity clothes for the pregnant women to wear so as to make them more distinguishable to the troops at the massacres, but, as you know, these people have their own ways and will not always consent to do even what is clearly in their own interest. And, of course, we have no intention of forcing them. That, after all, is why we are in Vietnam in the first place—to give these people the right to choose their own way of life, in accordance with *their* own beliefs and customs.

CITIZEN: In other words, sir, if Lieutenant Calley assumed the woman was simply fat, and killed her under that assumption, that would still square with your personal belief in the sanctity of human life, including the life of the yet unborn.

TRICKY: Absolutely. If I find that he assumed she was simply overweight, I give you my utmost assurance, I will in no way be prejudiced against his appeal.

CITIZEN: But, sir, suppose, just *suppose*, that he *did* know she was pregnant.

TRICKY: Well, we are down to the heart of the matter now, aren't we?

CITIZEN: I'm afraid so, sir.

TRICKY: Yes, we are down to this issue of 'abortion on demand,' which, admittedly, is totally unacceptable to me, on the basis of my personal and religious beliefs.

CITIZEN: Abortion on *demand*?

TRICKY: If this Vietnamese woman presented herself to Lieutenant Calley for abortion ... let's assume, for the sake of argument, she was one of those girls who goes out and has a good time and then won't own up to the consequences; unfortunately, we have them here just as they have them over there—the misfits, the bums, the tramps, the few who give the many a bad name ... but if this woman presented herself to Lieutenant Calley for abortion, with some kind of note, say, that somebody had written for her in English, and Lieutenant Calley, let's say, in the heat and pressure of the moment, performed the abortion, during the course of which the woman died ...

CITIZEN: Yes. I think I follow you so far.

14

TRICKY: Well, I just have to wonder if the woman isn't herself equally as guilty as the lieutenant—if she is not more so. I just have to wonder if this isn't a case for the Saigon courts, after all. Let's be perfectly frank: you cannot die of an abortion, if you don't go looking for the abortion to begin with. If you have not gotten yourself in an abortion *predicament* to begin with. Surely that's perfectly clear.

CITIZEN: It is, sir.

TRICKY: Consequently, even if Lieutenant Calley did participate in a case of 'abortion on demand,' it would seem to me, speaking strictly as a lawyer, mind you, that there are numerous extenuating factors to consider, not the least of which is the attempt to perform a surgical operation under battlefield conditions. I would think that more than one medic has been cited for doing less.

CITIZEN: Cited for what?

TRICKY: Bravery, of course.

CITIZEN: But ... but, Mr. President, what if it wasn't 'abortion on demand'? What if Lieutenant Calley gave her an abortion without her demanding one, or even asking for one— or even wanting one?

TRICKY: As an outright form of population control, you mean?

CITIZEN: Well, I was thinking more along the lines of an outright form of murder.

TRICKY (*reflecting*): Well, of course, that is a very iffy question, isn't it? What we lawyers call a hypothetical instance —isn't it? If you will remember, we are only *supposing* there to have been a pregnant woman in that ditch at My Lai to begin with. Suppose there *wasn't* a pregnant woman in that ditch—which, in fact, seems from all evidence to have been the case. We are then involved in a totally academic discussion.

CITIZEN: Yes, sir. If so, we are.

TRICKY: Which doesn't mean it hasn't been of great value to me, nonetheless. In my review of Lieutenant Calley's case, I will now be particularly careful to inquire whether there is so much as a single shred of evidence that one of those twenty-two in that ditch at My Lai was a pregnant woman. And if there is—if I should find in the evidence against the lieutenant anything whatsoever that I cannot square with my personal belief in the sanctity of human life, including the life of the yet unborn, I will disqualify myself as a judge and pass the entire matter on to the Vice President.

CITIZEN: Thank you, Mr. President. I think we can all sleep better at night knowing that.

TWO

TRICKY HOLDS A
PRESS CONFERENCE

MR. ASSLICK: Sir, as regards your San Dementia statement of April 3, the discussion it provoked seems now to have centered on your unequivocal declaration that you are a firm believer in the rights of the unborn. Many seem to believe that you are destined to be to the unborn what Martin Luther King was to the black people of America, and the late Robert F. Charisma to the disadvantaged chicanos and Puerto Ricans of the country. There are those who say that your San Dementia statement will go down in the history books alongside Dr. King's famous 'I have a dream' address. Do you find these comparisons apt?

TRICKY: Well, of course, Mr. Asslick, Martin Luther King was a very great man, as we all must surely recognize now that he is dead. He was a great leader in the struggle for equal rights for his people, and yes, I do believe he'll find a place in history. But of course we must not forget he was not the President of the United States, as I am, empowered by the Constitution, as I am; and this is an important distinction to bear in mind. Working *within* the Constitution I think I will be able to accomplish far more for the unborn of this *entire* nation than did Dr. King working *outside* the Constitution for the born of *a single race*. This is meant to be no criticism of Dr. King, but just a simple statement of fact.

Now, of course I am well aware that Dr. King died a martyr's tragic death—so let me then make one thing very clear to my enemies and the enemies of the unborn: let there be no mistake about it, what they did to Martin Luther King, what they did to Robert F. Charisma and to John F. Charisma before him, great Americans all, is not for a moment going to deter me from engaging in the struggle that lies ahead. I will not be intimidated by extremists or militants or violent fanatics from bringing justice and equality to those who live in the womb. And let me make one thing more perfectly clear: I am not just talking about the rights of the fetus. I am talking about the microscopic embryos as well. If ever there was a group in this country that was 'disadvantaged,' in the sense that they are utterly without representation or a voice in our national government, it is not the blacks or the Puerto Ricans or the hippies or what-have-you, all of whom have their spokesmen, but these infinitesimal creatures up there on the placenta.

You know, we all watch our TV and we see the demonstrators and we see the violence, because, unfortunately, that is the kind of thing that makes the news. But how many of us realize that throughout this great land of ours, there are millions upon millions of embryos going through the most complex and difficult changes in form and structure, and all this they accomplish without waving signs for the camera and disrupting traffic and throwing paint and using foul language and dressing in outlandish clothes. Yes, Mr. Daring.

MR. DARING: But what about those fetuses, sir, that the Vice President has labeled 'troublemakers'? I believe he was referring specifically to those who start in kicking around the fifth month. Do you agree that they are 'malcontents' and 'ingrates'? And if so, what measures do you intend to take to control them?

TRICKY: Well, first off, Mr. Daring, I believe we are dealing here with some very fine distinctions of a legal kind. Now, fortunately (*impish endearing smile*) I happen to be a lawyer and have the kind of training that enables me to make these fine distinctions. (*Back to serious business*) I think we have to be very very careful here—and I am sure the Vice President would agree with me—to distinguish between two kinds of activity: *kicking* in the womb, to which the Vice President was specifically referring, and *moving* in the womb. You see, the Vice President did not say, despite what you may

18

have heard on television, that *all* fetuses who are active in the womb are troublemakers. Nobody in this Administration believes that. In fact, I have just today spoken with both Attorney General Malicious and with Mr. Heehaw at the FBI, and we are all in agreement that a certain amount of movement in the womb, after the fifth month, is not only inevitable but *desirable* in a normal pregnancy.

But as for this other matter, I assure you, this administration does not intend to sit idly by and do nothing while American women are being kicked in the stomach by a bunch of violent five-month-olds. Now by and large, and I cannot emphasize this enough, our American unborn are as wonderful a group of unborn as you can find anywhere. But there are these violent few that the Vice President has characterized, and I don't think unjustly, in his own impassioned rhetoric, as 'troublemakers' and 'malcontents'—and the Attorney General has been instructed by me to take the appropriate action against them.

MR. DARING: If I may, sir, what sort of action will that be? Will there be arrests made of violent fetuses? And if so, how exactly will this be carried out?

TRICKY: I think I can safely say, Mr. Daring, that we have the finest law enforcement agencies in the world. I am quite sure that Attorney General Malicious can solve whatever procedural problems may arise. Mr. Respectful.

MR. RESPECTFUL: Mr. President, with all the grave national and international problems that press continually upon you, can you tell us why you have decided to devote yourself to this previously neglected issue of fetal rights? You seem pretty fired up on this issue, sir—why is that?

TRICKY: Because, Mr. Respectful, I will not tolerate injustice in any area of our national life. Because ours is a just society, not merely for the rich and the privileged, but for the most powerless among us as well. You know, you hear a lot these days about Black Power and Female Power, Power this and Power that. But what about Prenatal Power? Don't they have rights too, membranes though they may be? I for one think they do, and I intend to fight for them. Mr. Shrewd.

19

MR. SHREWD: As you must know, Mr. President, there are those who contend that you are guided in this matter solely by political considerations. Can you comment on that?

TRICKY: Well, Mr. Shrewd, I suppose that is their cynical way of describing my plan to introduce a proposed constitutional amendment that would extend the vote to the unborn in time for the '72 elections.

MR. SHREWD: I believe that is what they have in mind, sir. They contend that by extending the vote to the unborn you will neutralize the gains that may accrue to the Democratic Party by the voting age having been lowered to eighteen. They say your strategists have concluded that even if you should lose the eighteen-to-twenty-one-year-old vote, you can still win a second term if you are able to carry the South, the state of California, and the embryos and fetuses from coast to coast. Is there any truth to this 'political' analysis of your sudden interest in Prenatal Power?

TRICKY: Mr. Shrewd, I'd like to leave that to you—and to our television viewers—to judge, by answering your question in a somewhat personal manner. I assure you I am conversant with the opinions of the experts. Many of them are men whom I respect, and surely they have the right to say whatever they like, though of course one always hopes it will be in the national interest ... But let me remind you, and all Americans, because this is a fact that seems somehow to have been overlooked in this whole debate: I am no Johnny-come-lately to the problem of the rights of the unborn. The simple fact of the matter, and it is in the record for all to see, is that I myself was once unborn, in the great state of California. Of course, you wouldn't always know this from what you see on television or read in the papers (*impish endearing smile*) that some of you gentlemen write for, but it happens nonetheless to be the truth. (*Back to serious business*) I was an unborn Quaker, as a matter of fact.

And let me remind you—since it seems necessary to do so, in the face of the vicious and mindless attacks upon him—Vice President What's-his-name was also unborn once, an unborn Greek–American, and proud to have been one. We were just talking about that this morning, how he was once an unborn Greek–American, and all that has meant to him. And so too was Secretary Lard unborn and so was Secretary Codger unborn, and the Attorney General—why, I could go right on down through my cabinet and point out to you one fine man after another who was once unborn. Even Secretary Fickle, with whom as you know I had my differences of opinion, was unborn when he was here with us on the team.

And if you look among the leadership of the Republican Party in the House and the Senate, you will find men who long before their election to public office were unborn in just about every region of this country, on farms, in industrial cities, in small towns the length and breadth of this great republic. My own wife was once unborn. As you may recall, my children were both unborn.

So when they say that Dixon has turned to the issue of the unborn just for the sake of the votes ... well, I ask only that you consider this list of the previously unborn with whom I am associated in both public and private life, and decide for yourself. In fact, I think you are going to find, Mr. Shrewd, with each passing day, people around this country coming to realize that in this administration the fetuses and embryos of America have at last found their voice. Miss Charmin', I believe you had your eyebrows raised.

MISS CHARMIN': I was just going to say, sir, that of course President Lyin' B. Johnson was unborn, too, before he came to the White House—and he was a Democrat. Could you comment on that?

TRICKY: Miss Charmin', I would be the first to applaud my predecessor in this high office for having been unborn. I have no doubt that he was an outstanding fetus down there in Texas before he came into public life. I am not claiming that my administration is the first in history to be cognizant of the issue of fetal rights. I am saying that we intend to do something about them. Mr. Practical.

MR. PRACTICAL: Mr. President, I'd like to ask you to comment upon the scientific problems entailed in bringing the vote to the unborn.

21

TRICKY: Well, of course, Mr. Practical, you have hit the nail right on the head with the word 'scientific.' This is a scientific problem of staggering proportions—let's make no mistake about it. Moreover, I fully expect there are those who are going to say in tomorrow's papers that it is impossible, unfeasible, a utopian dream, and so on. But as you remember, when President Charisma came before the Congress in 1961, and announced that this country would put a man on the moon before the end of the decade, there were many who were ready to label him an impossible dreamer, too. But we did it. With American know-how and American teamwork, we did it. And so too do I have every confidence that our scientific and technological people are going to dedicate themselves to bringing the vote to the unborn—and not before the decade is out either, but before November of 1972.

MR. PRACTICAL: Can you give us some idea, sir, how much a crash program like this will cost?

TRICKY: Mr. Practical, I will be submitting a proposed budget to the Congress within the next ten days, but let me say this: you cannot achieve greatness without sacrifice. The program of research and development such as my scientific advisers have outlined cannot be bought 'cheap.' After all, what we are talking about here is nothing less than the fundamental principle of democracy: the vote. I cannot believe that the members of the Congress of the United States are going to play party politics when it comes to taking a step like this, which will be an advance not only for our nation, but for all mankind.

You just cannot imagine, for instance, the impact that this is going to have on the people in the under-developed countries. There are the Russians and the Chinese, who don't even allow adults to vote, and here we are in America, investing billions and billions of the taxpayers' dollars in a scientific project designed to extend the franchise to people who cannot see or talk or hear or even think, in the ordinary sense of the word. It would be a tragic irony indeed, and as telling a sign as I can imagine of national confusion and even hypocrisy, if we were willing to send our boys to fight and die in far-off lands so that defenseless peoples might have the right to choose the kinds of government they want in free elections, and then we were to turn around here at home and continue to deny that very same right to an entire segment of our population, just because they happen to live on the placenta or in the uterus, instead of New York City. Mr. Catch-Me-in-a-Contradiction.

MR. CATCH-ME-IN-A-CONTRADICTION: Mr. President, what startles me is that up until today you have been characterized, and not unwillingly, I think, as someone who, if he is not completely out of touch with the styles and ideas of the young, has certainly been skeptical of their wisdom. Doesn't this constitute, if I may use the word, a radical about-face, coming out now for the rights of those who are not simply 'young' but actually in the gestation period?

TRICKY: Well, I am glad you raised that point, because I think it shows once and for all just how flexible I am, and how I am always willing to listen and respond to an appeal from *any* minority group, no matter how powerless, just so long as it is reasonable, and is not accompanied by violence and foul language and throwing paint. If ever there was proof that you don't have to camp on the White House lawn to get the President's attention away from a football game, I think it is in the example of these little organisms. I tell you, they have really impressed me with their silent dignity and politeness. I only hope that all Americans will come to be as proud of our unborn as I am.

MR. FASCINATED: Mr. President, I am fascinated by the technological aspect. Can you give us just an inkling of how exactly the unborn will go about casting their ballots? I'm particularly fascinated by these embryos on the placenta, who haven't even developed nervous systems yet, let alone limbs such as we use in an ordinary voting machine.

TRICKY: Well, first off, let me remind you that nothing in our Constitution denies a man the right to vote just because he is physically handicapped. That isn't the kind of country we have here. We have many wonderful handicapped people in this country, but of course, they're not 'news' the way the demonstrators are.

MR. FASCINATED: I wasn't suggesting, sir, that just because these embryos don't have central nervous systems they should be denied the right to vote—I was thinking again of the fantastic *mechanics* of it. How, for instance, will the embryos be able to weigh the issues and make intelligent choices from among the candidates, if they are not able to read the newspapers or watch the news on television?

TRICKY: Well, it seems to me that you have actually touched upon the very strongest claim that the unborn have for enfranchisement, and why it is such a crime they have been denied the vote for so long. Here, at long last, we have a great bloc of voters who simply are not going to be taken in by the lospided and distorted versions of the truth that are presented to the American public through the various media. Mr. Reasonable.

MR. REASONABLE: But how then will they make up their minds, or their yolks, or their nuclei, or whatever it is they have in there, Mr. President? It might seem to some that they are going to be absolutely innocent of whatever may be at stake in the election.

TRICKY: Innocent they will be, Mr. Reasonable—but now let me ask you, and all our television viewers, too, a question: what's *wrong* with a little innocence? We've had the foul language, we've had the cynicism, we've had the masochism and the breast-beating—maybe a big dose of innocence is just what this country needs to be great again.

MR. REASONABLE: *More* innocence, Mr. President?

TRICKY: Mr. Reasonable, if I have to choose between the rioting and the upheaval and the strife and the discontent on the one hand, and more innocence on the other, I think I will choose the innocence. Mr. Hardnose.

MR. HARDNOSE: In the event, Mr. President, that all this does come to pass by the '72 elections, what gives you reason to believe that the enfranchised embryos and fetuses will vote for you over your Democratic opponent? And what about Governor Wallow? Do you think that if he should run again, he would significantly cut into your share of the fetuses, particularly in the South?

TRICKY: Let me put it this way, Mr. Hardnose: I have the utmost respect for Governor George Wallow of Alabama, as I do for Senator Hubert Hollow of Minnesota. They are both able men, and they speak with great conviction, I am sure, in behalf of the extreme right and the extreme left. But the fact is that I have never heard either of these gentlemen, for all their extremism, raise their voices in behalf of America's most disadvantaged group of all, the unborn.

Consequently, I would be less than candid if I didn't say that when election time rolls around, of course the embryos and fetuses of this country are likely to remember just who it was that struggled in their behalf, while others were addressing themselves to the more popular and fashionable issues of the day. I think they will remember who it was that devoted himself, in the midst of a war abroad and racial crisis at home, to making this country a fit place for the unborn to dwell in pride.

My only hope is that whatever I am able to accomplish in their behalf while I hold this office will someday contribute to a world in which *everybody*, regardless of race, creed or color, will be unborn. I guess if *I* have a dream, that is it. Thank you, ladies and gentlemen.

MR. ASSLICK: Thank you, Mr. President.

THREE

TRICKY HAS ANOTHER CRISIS;
OR, THE SKULL SESSION

Tricky is dressed in the football uniform he wore during his four years on the bench at Prissier College. It is still as spanking new as the day it was issued to him some forty years ago, despite the fact that when he finds himself at night so perplexed and anguished by the burdens of the Presidency as to be unable to fall off to sleep, he frequently rises from his bed and steals down through the White House to the blast-proof underground locker room (built under his direction to specifications furnished by the Baltimore Colts and the Atomic Energy Commission) and 'suits up,' as though for 'the big game' against Prissier's 'traditional rival.' And invariably, as during the Cambodian incursion and the Kent State killings, simply to don shoulder guards, cleats and helmet, to draw the snug football pants up over his leather athletic supporter and then to turn his back to the mirror and catch a peek over his big shoulders at the number on his back, is enough to restore his faith in the course of action he has taken in behalf of two hundred million Americans. Indeed, even in the midst of the most incredible international blunders and domestic catastrophes, he has till now, with the aid of his football uniform, and a good war movie, been able to live up to his own description of the true leader in Six Hundred Crises as 'cool, confident and decisive.' 'What is essential in such situations,' he wrote there, summarizing what he had learned about leadership from the riots inspired by his 1958 visit, as Vice President, to Caracas, 'is not so much "bravery" in the face of danger as the ability to think "selflessly"—to blank out any thought of personal fear by concentrating completely on how

26

to meet the danger.'

But tonight not even barking signals at the full-length mirror and pretending to fade back, arm cocked, to spot a downfield receiver (while being charged by the opposing line) has he been able to blank out thoughts of personal fear; and as for thinking 'selflessly,' he has not been making much headway in that department either. Having run plays before the mirror for two full hours—having completed eighty-seven out of one hundred attempted forward passes for a total of two thousand six hundred and ten yards gained in the air in one night (a White House record)—he is nonetheless unable to concentrate on how to meet the danger before him, and so has decided to awaken his closest advisers and summon them to the underground locker room for what is known in football parlance as a 'skull session.'

At the door to the White House, each has been issued a uniform by a Secret Service agent, disguised, but for a shoulder holster, as an ordinary locker room attendant in sweat pants, sneakers and T-shirt stenciled 'Property of the White House.' Now, seated on benches before the big blackboard, the 'coaches' listen carefully as Tricky, with his helmet in his hands, describes to them the crisis he is having trouble being entirely selfless about.

TRICKY: I don't understand it. How can these youngsters be saying what they are saying about me? How can they be chanting those slogans, waving those signs—about *me*? Gentlemen, by all reports they are growing more surly and audacious by the hour. By morning we may have on our hands the most incredible upheaval in history: a revolution by the Boy Scouts of America! (*In an attempt to calm himself, and become confident and decisive, he puts on his helmet*)

Now it was one thing when those Vietnam soreheads came down here to the Capitol to turn their medals in. Everybody knew they were just a bunch of malcontents who had lost arms and legs and so on, and so had nothing better to do with their time than hobble around feeling sorry for themselves. Of course they couldn't be objective about the war—half of them were in wheelchairs because of it. But what we have now isn't just a mob of ingrates—these are *the Boy Scouts*!

And don't you think for one moment that the American people are going to sit idly by when a Boy Scout, an *Eagle Scout*, climbs to the top of the Capitol steps and calls the President of the United States 'a dirty old man.' Let there be no mistake about it, if we do not deal with these angry Scouts as coolly and confidently and decisively as I dealt with Khrushchev in that kitchen, by tomorrow I will be the first President in American history to be even more hated and despised than Lyin' B. Johnson. Gentlemen, you can go to war without Congressional consent, you can ruin the economy and trample on the Bill of Rights, but you just do not violate the moral code of the Boy Scouts of America and expect to be reelected to the highest office in the land!

And yet when I made that speech at San Dementia, it all seemed so ... so perfectly and, if I may say so, so brilliantly, innocuous. Five minutes later I didn't even remember what it was I'd *endorsed*. That my political opponents could now be so desperate to oust me from power—so disrespectful, not simply of me, but of the august office of the Presidency, to take those few utterly harmless and totally meaningless words that I spoke that day, and turn them into this monstrous lie!

Gentlemen, I am no newcomer to the ugly game of politics. I have seen all kinds of chicanery and deceit in my day—falsification, misquotation, distortion, embellishment and, of course, outright suppression of the truth. Nor am I what you would call a babe-in-the-woods when it comes to the techniques of character assassination. Years ago I looked on in disgust and horror when they crucified Senator Joseph McCatastrophy just because he kept changing his mind as to the number of Communists there were in the State Department. I saw what they did only recently to Judge Carswell. I saw what they did to Judge Haynsworth. Why, just last month look what they tried to do to Secretary Lard, when he held up that phony piece of pipe before the Senate Foreign Relations Committee and said it was from Laos instead of Vietnam. Five miles away—and they're ready to hang him for it!

But, I must admit, never in my long career of dealing with falsehood have I come upon a lie so treacherous and Machiavellian as this one my enemies are trying to pass off about me ... *What did I say?* Let's look at the record. I said *nothing! Absolutely nothing!* I came out for 'the rights of the unborn.' I mean if ever there was a line of hokum, that was it. Sheer humbug! And as if it wasn't clear enough what I was up to, I even tacked on, 'as recognized in principles expounded by the United Nations.' *By the United Nations.* Now what more could I possibly have said to make the whole thing any more inane? Maybe I was supposed to have told them 'as recognized in principles expounded by the American Automobile Association.' Maybe I should have given the whole speech in Pig Latin, and made funny faces while I was at it! Maybe I should have come out to make the statement in a clown's costume! But I did not do that—because I refuse to talk down to the American public. I refuse to pull my punches. I refuse to believe that the people of this great nation are incapable of recognizing the most outrageous kind of hypocrisy or sniffing out the most blatant contradictions imaginable ... And yet this, *this* is my reward, for my faith in America. The Boy Scouts of America screaming to the TV cameras that Trick E. Dixon favors sexual intercourse. Favors fornication—*between people!*

POLITICAL COACH: Of course, as of now, it's still only the Boy Scouts, Mr. President.

TRICKY: Today the Boy Scouts (*here he sinks down onto the bench before the blackboard, barely restraining a sob*)—tomorrow the world! ... And what about my wife—what is she going to think? What if *she* starts to believe it? *What about my children?* WHAT ABOUT THE VOTERS!

SPIRITUAL COACH: Here, here, Mr. President. I sympathize with your chagrin, particularly as it relates to your fine family. But, frankly, I do not believe that the American people who see you on TV, any more than those who know you at first-hand, are going to be taken in by such a blatant fabrication. If ever a man, in his every word and deed, his every movement and gesture, his glance, his sneer, his very smile, put the lie to

29

such a slanderous accusation as this one, it is you.

TRICKY (*visibly moved*): Reverend, I thank you for that tribute. Surely I have tried to give no indication whatsoever to the people of this country that I even know what sexual intercourse *is*. Furthermore, I have instructed my family that they must under no circumstances allow it to appear that any of us have ever in our lives been infected by desire or lust, or, for that matter, an appetite for anything at all, outside of political power. This may sound immodest of me, but I happen to pride myself on the fact that if it weren't for my perspiring so on television, the American people would probably have no way in the world of telling that under my clothes I am flesh. And, of course you all know, as a result of a decision I reached here during a lonely vigil in the locker room only a few nights ago, this disorder will very shortly be corrected when I enter Walter Reed Hospital to undergo a secret operation for the surgical removal of the sweat glands from my upper lip. You see, gentlemen, that is how dedicated I am to dissociating myself from anything remotely *resembling* a human body.

But now to accuse me of *this*! As though to be for the rights of the unborn was prima facie evidence—that is, evidence sufficient to establish a fact, or to raise a presumption of fact ... that's what we lawyers mean by that phrase ... as you know, before entering the White House I was a lawyer, and so I know phrases like that ... as though that were prima facie evidence that I was also in favor of the process by which the unborn come into existence in the first place. To accuse me, because of a perfectly innocuous statement like that, of encouraging people to have intercourse in order that they should have unborn, in order that those unborn should have these rights—that don't even exist! And that I wouldn't care about, even if they did! How could I? Here I am, President of the United States and Leader of the Free World, working and slaving with every fiber of my being, night and day, three hundred and sixty-five days a year, for the sole purpose of getting myself reelected—where would I find the time to worry about the rights of *anything*? Haven't they any idea what this job is all about? The whole thing is so patently absurd! And yet there are those Boy Scouts, in uniform, marching in the streets of the nation's capital—and those signs:

GO BACK TO CALIFORNIA, SENSUALIST, WHERE YOU BELONG

POWER TO THE PENIS? NEVER!

REPRESSION—LOVE IT OR LEAVE IT!

SPIRITUAL COACH (*solemnly, taking the arm of the shaken President*): Mr. President, forgive them, they know not what their signs say.

TRICKY: Oh, Reverend, Reverend, I assure you, under ordinary circumstances I would bend over *backwards* to forgive them. I like to think that I am the kind of man who can find it in his heart to forgive his worst enemy. Why, not only have I forgiven Alger Hiss, but when I was elected President, I sent him an anonymous telegram expressing my gratitude for all he had done in my behalf. And that man was a *perjurer*! Listen, I would actually have forgiven Khrushchev himself, yes, right there in that kitchen, if it had been politically expedient to do so. Just look what I'm up to right now: I'm in the very process of forgiving Mao Tse-tung, who by my own estimate has enslaved *six hundred million people*!

But I am afraid, Reverend, that where these Boy Scouts are concerned, we are fighting for a principle so fundamental to civilized life, that even a man of my magnanimity must rise up and say 'No, this time you have gone too far.' Reverend, *they are trying to prevent me from winning a second term*!

SPIRITUAL COACH: I see ... I see ... I must confess that I had not thought of it quite that way.

TRICKY: It is not a pleasant way to *have* to think about it. All of us would prefer to look with charity and respect upon our fellow human beings, whatever their race, creed, color or age, and to treat them according to the tenets of our religious beliefs. Certainly no one in this country wishes to appear more

31

religious than I do. But sometimes, Reverend, people just make being religious impossible, even for someone who stands to gain as much from that posture as I do.

SPIRITUAL COACH: But if such is the case, if these Boy Scouts, for some incomprehensible reason, are out to destroy your political career by casting doubt upon your Sunday school morality, perhaps it would be best for you to go on television and give the people the facts as they really are. As you did when they accused you in the 1952 election of being the recipient of an illegal political fund. The Checkers Speech.

TRICKY (*intrigued*): You mean give it again?

SPIRITUAL COACH: Well, perhaps not the *very* same speech.

TRICKY: Why not? It worked.

SPIRITUAL COACH: True. But I wonder, Mr. President, if it addresses directly the issue at hand.

TRICKY: Maybe not. But you know, Reverend, when you're dealing with wild and reckless charges like these, when you're in the midst of a crisis such as this one, that could snowball overnight into political *disaster*, then you sometimes have to do what works, and leave things like the issues themselves for later. Otherwise, I'm afraid there might not *be* any later.

SPIRITUAL COACH: Well, I'm not a politician, Mr. President, and I must admit that I may be hopelessly naive to believe that The Truth Shall Make Ye Free. But I do think that if instead of giving the Checkers Speech again, instead of itemizing your earnings over the years and telling how much money you owe your parents and so on, you were now to make a *similar* address, in which you presented to the nation an itemized account of your sexual experiences, giving exact dates from your appointment calendar—when, where and with whom—you might well feel secure in leaving it to the American people to judge whether or not you are an advocate of fornication.

TRICKY: You mean, go on TV *with* the appointment books . . .

SPIRITUAL COACH: Yes, and leaf through them page by page, until at last you come upon an item to read aloud. I would think the long silences will in themselves be the most eloquent part of the broadcast.

TRICKY: What about charts though? What about a graph? You see, I don't know if people are going to sit around all night in front of their television sets waiting for me to say something. But if we had a graph where we measured the hours in which I have engaged in the ordinary human activities of scheming, plotting, smearing and so on, against those I've spent having intercourse—well, it could be pretty impressive.

And I could use a pointer! At the risk of seeming immodest, I think I can hold my own with any schoolmaster in the country in using a pointer and charts, though of course by training I'm a lawyer, you know ... And I'll borrow a dog!

Well, how does it sound to the rest of you?

POLITICAL COACH: Speaking frankly, Mr. President, I think we are barking up the wrong tree with this whole idea of using the truth *or* the dog. We've used the dog, of course, and with some success, and though I don't have my file with me, I'm sure we've used the truth some time or other in the past, too. Off the top of my head I can't remember exactly when, but if you like I'll have my secretary look it up in the morning. However, right now it seems to me that, given the hysteria of those Scouts, and the kind of coverage they're getting, if you were to go on television and say that you have had intercourse only *once* in your entire life, maybe as some kind of initiation rite when you were in the Navy—crossing the equator maybe—and that the whole thing had lasted less than sixty seconds, and you had hated it from beginning to end, and that you had to be held down throughout, and so on, even that would be enough to make you appear guilty of the charges the Boy Scouts are bringing against you.

TRICKY (*reflecting*): Of course, if you're going to rule out the dog and the truth and so on, maybe the best approach is for me to go on TV and deny the whole thing. Say I've *never* had intercourse.

POLITICAL COACH (*shaking his head*): Have you seen that mob, Mr. President? They wouldn't believe you, not at this point.

TRICKY: Suppose I spoke from HEW, with the Surgeon General at my side, and he read a medical report stating that I am not now, nor have I ever been in the past, capable of performing coitus.

SPIRITUAL COACH: Mr. President, at the risk of being politically naive again, you *are* the father of two children ... that is, if that means anything, in this context ...

POLITICAL COACH: Politically naive, hell—that was good thinking, Reverend.

TRICKY: But why can't we just say they were adopted?

POLITICAL COACH: No, no, that doesn't really solve the problem. Even if we are able to establish you as not only sterile, but one hundred percent impotent, even if we were able to get the American public to believe that these children who resemble you so were adopted—and, mind you, I think we could do both, if it came down to it—you are still going to be compromised, it would seem to me, by appearing to have taken into your home the offspring of somebody *else's* sexual intercourse. You are still going to be locked into this fornication issue.

LEGAL COACH: Absolutely. Open-and-shut case of guilt by association. If I were the judge, I'd throw the book at you. And another objection. If he goes on TV and says he's impotent, most of the people out there aren't even going to know what he's talking about. I don't doubt that half of them are going to think that he means he's queer.

POLITICAL COACH: Wait a minute! Wait *one* minute! How about it, Mr. President?

TRICKY: How about what?

POLITICAL COACH: Going on TV and saying you're queer. Would you do it?'

TRICKY: Oh, I'll do it, all right, if you think it'll work.

SPIRITUAL COACH: Oh, but *surely*, Mr. President ...

TRICKY: Reverend, we are talking about *my political career*! With all due respect, we happen now to be listening to a man whose *business* is politics, just the way yours is religion, and if he says that in a situation like this one the truth and the dog and so on are not going to get us anywhere, then I must assume he knows what he is talking about. After all, one of the signs of a great leader is his willingness to listen to all sides of an issue without being blinded by his own prejudices and preconceptions. Now I am a Quaker, as you well know, and consequently it is only natural that I should be prejudiced in behalf of the advice given to me by a spiritual person like yourself. But I cannot run from the facts, just so as to be a better Quaker in your eyes and in mine. We are dealing with a mob of youngsters whose minds have been poisoned with a terrible lie. We are going to have to find a way to restore them to their senses while simultaneously restoring to the office of the Presidency its dignity and prestige. And if in order to accomplish those two important tasks I have to go on TV and say I am a homosexual, then I will do it. I had the courage to call Alger Hiss a Communist. I had the courage to call Khrushchev a bully. I assure you, I have the courage now to call myself a queer!

The problem is not my courage to say this or say that; it never has been. The problem, as always, is one of credibility. Will they believe me?

General, will they buy it over at the Pentagon? That should certainly be a good test case.

MILITARY COACH (*considering*): They might, sir. They very well might.

TRICKY: Would it help if I batted my eyes more, when I talk?

MILITARY COACH: No, no, I think they feel you bat your eyes enough already, sir. Any more and it might not go over too well with some of the old-timers.

TRICKY: I take it from what you say that you would positively rule out my wearing a dress. Something simple. A basic black, say.

MILITARY COACH: Not necessary, sir.

TRICKY: How about earrings?

MILITARY COACH: No, I think you're fine as you are, sir.

TRICKY: The point is I don't want to come off as just a sissy. Five o'clock shadow and all, I really have to watch myself in that department.

35

SPIRITUAL COACH: Mr. President, if I may, in your eagerness to do the right thing for the nation, I think you may be overlooking a small technical point. Homosexuals have intercourse also.

TRICKY (*stunned*): They do? ... *How?* (*Here the Spiritual Coach takes Tricky by the hand—much as he might comfort one in bereavement—and, leaning forward, discreetly whispers the answer into the President's ear*)

TRICKY (*recoiling*): Why, that's awful! That's disgusting! You're making that up!

SPIRITUAL COACH: Would that I were, Mr. President.

TRICKY: But—but—(*Here he leans forward to whisper into the Reverend's ear*)

SPIRITUAL COACH: I suppose they don't care about that, Mr. President.

TRICKY (*outraged*): But that's bestial! That's monstrous! This is America! And I'm the *President* of America! And—and—(*turning in bewilderment to the other coaches*) listen, do you people realize what's going *on* in this country? Do you know what he just *told* me?

POLITICAL COACH: I think we do, Mr. President.

TRICKY: But that's *grotesque*! Uccchhy! It makes my lip crawl!

POLITICAL COACH: To be sure, Mr. President. But nonetheless in terms of the problem that is facing us, it happens to be neither here nor there. The point is this: homosexuals, regardless of whatever else they may do, are in no way involved in the sort of sexual activity that produces fetuses—and that is still what these Boy Scouts are up in arms about. Consequently, if you were to go on TV and say you were a homosexual, in the minds of most Americans you would have cleared yourself of the charge the Boy Scouts are making, that you are a heterosexual activist. You'll be entirely in the clear.

TRICKY: I see ... I see ... Okay—I'll do it! There—*that's* the way to be in a crisis: decisive! Just as I wrote in my book, summarizing what I learned during General Poppapower's heart attacks, 'Decisive action relieves the tension which builds up in a crisis. When the situation requires that an individual

36

restrain himself from acting decisively over a long period, this can be the most wearing of all crises.'

You see, it isn't even what you decide—it's *that* you decide. Otherwise there's that darn tension; too much, and, I tell you, a person could probably crack up. And I for one will not crack up while I am President of the United States. I want that to be perfectly clear. If you read my book, you'll see that my entire career has been devoted to not cracking up, as much as to anything. And I don't intend to start now. Cool, confident and decisive. I'll do it—I'll say I'm a queer!

LEGAL COACH: I wouldn't if I were you, Mr. President.

TRICKY: You *wouldn't*?

LEGAL COACH: Nope, not if I were the President of the United States. Why should you? At the time of the Checkers Speech, when you were only a candidate for the Vice Presidency, of course it was necessary to explain and apologize and be humble and tell them how much money you owed your Mommy and Daddy and that you had a doggie and so on. Look, I wouldn't have objected back then if you had gotten down on your hands and knees on television, and demeaned and debased yourself in whatever way was most natural to you, in order to come to power. But now you are *in* power. Now you *are* the President. And who are those kids in the street, leveling these outlandish charges at you? They're kids, in a street. I don't care what kind of uniforms they wear, they are still not adults in houses. And that makes all the difference in the world.

TRICKY: Your suggestion then is what?

LEGAL COACH: No less than any other citizen in this country, Mr. President, you still have recourse to the law. I say use it. I say round 'em up, put 'em in the clink, and throw the key away.

MILITARY COACH: Objection! Enough mollycoddling of the enemy. Let's get it over with once and for all. Shoot 'em!

TRICKY (*considering*): Interesting idea. I mean that is just about as decisive as you can get, isn't it? But may I ask, General, shoot 'em *after* we round 'em up, or *before*? This of course is the problem we always have, isn't it?

37

MILITARY COACH: *After*, sir, and we are running the same old risk.

LEGAL COACH: On the other hand, General, *before* and don't think you aren't running a risk too. *Before*, and I can tell you now, sure as we're sitting here, you are going to get those civil-rights nuts down on your neck, and I tell you they are a great big pain in the ass to everybody involved, and can tie up my staff for days at a time.

MILITARY COACH: Granted, they are a nuisance. But *after*, and you are going to get yourself mired down with these Boy Scouts just the way we are mired down in Southeast Asia. *After*, and you are sacrificing what is fundamental to the success of any attack: the element of surprise. Common sense tells us that even the enemy is not so stupid as to stand around waiting to be shot, but if he has had sufficient warning that he is about to be killed, will take some kid of cowardly and, often enough, vicious means of protecting his life, such as fighting back. Now I, of course, abhor that kind of deviousness as much as anyone; nonetheless we must face up to it: these people haven't the slightest sense of fair play, and many of them will not even stand still waiting around to be jailed, let alone killed.

And what about the *moral* issue? I have a conscience to live with, gentlemen, I have a tradition to uphold, I am responsible to something more important than dollars and cents. And I tell you, I will not mollycoddle the enemy at the risk of American lives, unless of course I am ordered to do so. Mr. President, I must speak from my heart, I would be remiss as a General of the United States Army if I did not. Mr. President, if on the day you took office we had, with your permission, lined up and shot every single Vietnamese we could find, by so doing we would have saved fifteen thousand American lives. Instead, sir, following the course of action that you have ordered as Commander-in-Chief, and shooting and blowing them up piecemeal, catch as catch can, ten here, twenty there, and so on, we have suffered severe losses of both men and materials.

Admittedly, by doggedly pursuing your strategy, we are now beginning to see some light at the end of the tunnel. And

I have every hope that we will be able to help you make good on your promise to the American people, that by Election Day 1972, and according to your own secret timetable, you will have accomplished the complete withdrawal of the Vietnamese people from Vietnam.

My point, sir, is that we have ways of accomplishing such withdrawals in a matter of hours. I beg of you, Mr. President, let us not repeat the errors of Vietnam in our own backyard.

LEGAL COACH: Of course, Mr. President, I cannot fault the General on his tactical wisdom, and believe me, I am not for a moment worried about taking on these civil-rights nuts. It's just that if we shoot these Scouts in the street *before* we round 'em up and jail 'em, it is, as I said, going to create an awful lot of unnecessary busy-work for my staff, many of them first-rate young men whom I can employ at far more useful and worthwhile tasks.

However, before *or* after, Mr. President, whichever you choose, you can count on my support. But for you to go on TV and make a confession, or an apology, or any kind of explanation for yourself *whatsoever*, well, to my mind, nothing could more seriously undermine your moral and political authority, or constitute a graver threat to the cause of law and order. I will even go so far as to say that if you appear in any way to give ground on this issue—or *any* issue for that matter—you will be opening the floodgates to anarchy, socialism, communism, welfarism, defeatism, pacifism, perversion, pornography, prostitution, mob rule, drug addiction, free love, alcoholism and desecration of the flag. You'll see a rise just in jaywalking that will stagger the imagination. Now I don't mean to throw a scare into anyone, but the fact is a vast criminal element in this country is waiting for just a single sign of weakness in our leader, so as to make its move. Anything at all that might suggest to them that Trick E. Dixon is not totally in control, of himself *and* the nation, and I hate to tell you what would follow.

TRICKY (*interrupting*): That's exactly why I'm having my sweat glands removed, to show how in control I am.

LEGAL COACH (*continuing*): Now, as you know, there is

bound to be a certain amount of blood shed, when we go ahead and kill these young people, whether we do it before *or* after. This blood is something we seem always to run into with the killings, one of those facts of death we have to live with. Reverend, I see you shaking your head. Are you suggesting that it is possible to kill people, even youngsters like this, without spilling blood? If so, I'd like to hear about it.

SPIRITUAL COACH (*anguished*): Well ... what about gas ... poison gas ... Something like that? Surely enough blood has been shed in our century.

MILITARY COACH: The only trouble with gas, Reverend, if I may speak here on the basis of my own firsthand experience— the trouble with gas is that unfortunately we don't have these Scouts in a big open space. If we had them, say, smack in the middle of a desert somewhere, sure, spray 'em and it's over with.

SPIRITUAL COACH: Couldn't we *get* them to a desert then?

LEGAL COACH: How? (*Wary*) Are you suggesting bussing them there?

SPIRITUAL COACH: Well, yes, busses would do it, I suppose.

TRICKY: No, I'm afraid they wouldn't, Reverend. I have thought this matter through and I have made my decision: this administration will *not* bus children from Washington, D.C., all the way to the state of Arizona to poison them. That is a matter in which the federal government simply will not intervene. This is a free country, and certainly one of your fundamental freedoms here is choosing the place where you want your child to be killed.

SPIRITUAL COACH: And there's simply no way you can poison them right *here*?

MILITARY COACH: Much too dangerous, Reverend. Start out gassing these kids, and next thing, you get a wind or something, and you have poisoned some perfectly innocent adult miles away.

LEGAL COACH: Of course, you're going to get some guilty adults too, you know, if you let it spread far enough.

SPIRITUAL COACH: Gentlemen, please! I stand utterly opposed to any course of action wherein the welfare of a single innocent adult is even remotely threatened. I don't care how many guilty adults you get in the process.

MILITARY COACH: All right with me, Reverend. I'd rather shoot 'em anyway. I have always maintained that it gives the individual soldier a stronger sense of participation and accomplishment to pull the trigger and see the results with his own eyes.

SPIRITUAL COACH (*to Legal Coach*): And you?

LEGAL COACH: Fine with me. So long as we all realize beforehand that there is going to be this blood, and sure as we are sitting here, the media are going to exploit it to the hilt. I don't have any doubt whatsoever, given the kind of people who pull the strings in the press and TV, that they are going to blow this whole thing out of proportion, and, for instance, are not going to have a word to say about the restraint that's been displayed by our not using poison gas, or bussing. I mean, we could subject these kids to what is virtually a cross-country bus trip, a long hot grueling drive out to Arizona, without food, water, toilet facilities and so on, prior to killing them, and yet, as we all know, with the exception of the Reverend here, not a single member of the administration has spoken in support of such a proposal. But will you hear about that on TV? I think not.

TRICKY: Oh no. They never tell *that* side of the story. It's not *sensational* enough for them, not enough *gore*. Not enough *violence* to suit their taste. No, it's never what we didn't do, it's always what we've *done*. That, unfortunately, is what these people consider newsworthy.

LEGAL COACH: Luckily, Mr. President, the people of this country are still by and large passive and indifferent enough not to get all stirred up by this kind of irresponsible sensationalism on the part of the media.

TRICKY: Oh, don't get me wrong. I've never lost my faith in the wonderful indifference of the American people. Just because they happen to see a little Boy Scout blood on TV ... *Boy Scout blood on TV?* (*His lip is suddenly drenched with perspiration*) They'll impeach me! They'll——!

LEGAL COACH: Nothing of the sort, Mr. President, nothing

of the sort. It's only another crisis, you have nothing to worry about. Come on now—cool, confident and decisive. Come on, repeat it after me, you know how to behave in a crisis: cool, confident and decisive.

TRICKY: Cool, confident and decisive. Cool, confident and decisive. Cool, confident and decisive. Cool, confident and decisive.

LEGAL COACH: Feel better now? Crisis over?

TRICKY: I think so, yes.

LEGAL COACH: You see, you mustn't be frightened of Boy Scouts, Mr. President. Of course they're going to bleed a little and there may even be this hue and cry about it on TV, but when the country sees this sign that one of them was carrying before the bleeding began (*extracts from his briefcase a sign reading* DIXON FAVORS EFFING—*The Reverend gasps*), I think our worries are going to be over. Let the newspapers run all the photos of Boy Scouts corpses they want— we'll just run a photo of this sign, and of the five thousand replicas that I have asked the Government Printing Office to run off by morning. We'll see who gets the support of the nation then.

TRICKY: Look! I've stopped sweating!

LEGAL COACH: See? You've weathered another crisis, Mr. President.

TRICKY: Wow! That makes six hundred and *one*! (*Congratulations all around, from everyone except the Highbrow Coach, who speaks now for the first time*)

HIGHBROW COACH: Gentlemen, I wonder if I may take a somewhat different approach to the problem that we have been assembled here to solve. All the while I have been listening to your suggestions, I have simultaneously been bringing to bear upon the problem all my brainpower, wisdom, academic credentials, cunning, opportunism, love of power and so on, and the result is this list that I am holding in my hand, of the names of five individuals and/or organizations upon whom I think we can safely—if I may use the vernacular for a moment—pin the rap.

LEGAL COACH (*his interest suddenly aroused, after initial suspiciousness of 'the Professor'*): The rap?

HIGHBROW COACH: 'The rap.'

LEGAL COACH: Which rap?

HIGHBROW COACH: You name it. Inciting to riot. Tampering with the morals of minors. If you prefer, corrupting the youth of the nation.

POLITICAL COACH: 'Corrupting the youth.' Hey, that's got a real campaign ring to it!

HIGHBROW COACH: And a certain historical resonance, I would think.

SPIRITUAL COACH: At the risk of sounding 'square,' may I put in a good word for 'tampering with the morals of minors'? I've always found it to have tremendous appeal. It seems there is something in the word 'tampering' that particularly infuriates people.

LEGAL COACH: That may be, Reverend, but in my book you still can't beat 'inciting to riot' for scaring the hell out of the public.

TRICKY: And you, General! You look distressed again.

MILITARY COACH: I *am* distressed again! I am distressed every time the Professor opens his mouth! What is this business of bringing charges? Oh, mind you, they're good charges and I don't have anything against them personally, but the last thing I remember we were talking about shooting the bastards.

HIGHBROW COACH: General, despite your low opinion of intellectuals, I happen to have the highest regard for Army officers such as yourself, particularly in their devotion to their men and to their country. I wonder if once you have heard me read my list, you won't agree that to charge any of these five self-avowed enemies of America with the crime, to fix the responsibility for the uprising of the Boy Scouts on any one of them, will simultaneously absolve the Boy Scouts themselves of any real guilt, while totally discrediting the charges they have made against the President. The Scouts will retreat in panic . . .

MILITARY COACH: But without our firing a shot!

HIGHBROW COACH: The country isn't going away, General.

TRICKY: Sounds interesting, Professor. But why only one of the five? That strikes me as highly unusual.

HIGHBROW COACH: Well, perhaps, but I was just wondering if we haven't gone the route with the conspiracy business.

TRICKY: Oh, but it's so much fun when you get to choose two or three. Each person picks his favorites—and then all the wheeling and dealing, until we come up with the conspiracy that suits everybody.

LEGAL COACH: And, of course, Mr. President, to put in a word here in behalf of the cause of justice, the more choice you're allowed, the greater the chance of catching the right culprit. My feeling is that just to stay on the safe side, each of us should choose a minimum of three.

SPIRITUAL COACH: I know I'm outside my bailiwick again, but if it *is* going to improve the chances for justice being done, why can't we choose all *five*?

MILITARY COACH: Mr. President, I am growing more and more exasperated by the moment. Here we sit, in the comfort and splendor of this fully equipped underground locker room, in full football regalia, deliberating over the niceties of justice, while, with every passing moment, those Boy Scouts are readying themselves for battle against my men. I think it is high time we reminded the Professor that he is no longer up there in his ivory tower, where you can talk yourself blue in the face about this one's rights and that one's rights and how many rights fit on the head of a pin. There is an angry mob of Boy Scouts out there, Eagle Scouts among them, and they are growing angrier and more threatening by the moment. I say shoot 'em and shoot 'em now!

TRICKY: General, you are a brave soldier and a loyal American. But, I must say, I sense in your remarks a certain disregard for fundamental constitutional liberties such as I have pledged myself to uphold in my oath of office.

MILITARY COACH: Mr. President, I have the highest regard for the Constitution. If I didn't, I wouldn't have devoted my life to fighting to defend it. But the fact of the matter is, we are playing with a time bomb. Right now it is still only the Boy Scouts. By morning, and I can guarantee you this, their ranks are going to be infiltrated by dissolute Brownies and Cub Scouts looking for adventure. Now it's one thing to ask my men to mow down Eagle Scouts; it is another for them to have to deal with little boys and girls half that size. Those kids can run like the dickens, and they're *small*. As a result, what right now would still be a routine street massacre, will be converted into dangerous house-to-house fighting, in which we are bound to sustain heavy losses by way of our soldiers shooting mistakenly at each other.

TRICKY: I think you know, General, that nobody wants to save the lives of our boys—by that I mean, of course, our men—any more than I do. But I repeat: I will not do so by trampling upon the Constitution. I campaigned for this office as a strict constructionist where the Constitution of this country is concerned, and if I were now to take the course that you suggest and acted to prevent this group from voting in open and honest elections on the Professor's list, then the American people would have every right to throw me out of office tomorrow.

And let me make one thing perfectly clear: nobody is ever going to do that again. They have thrown me out of office enough in my lifetime! I will not be cast in the role of a loser—of a war, or of *anything*. And if that means bringing the full firepower of our Armed Forces to bear upon every last Brownie and Cub Scout in America, then that is what we are going to do. Because the President of the United States and Leader of the Free World can ill-afford to be humiliated by *anyone*, let alone by third- and fourth-graders who have nothing better to do than engage the United States Army in treacherous house-to-house combat. I don't care if we have to go into the nursery schools. I don't care if our men have to fight their way through barricades constructed of lanyards and hula hoops and bubble gum, under a steady barrage of toys being grossly misused as weapons—I, as Commander-in-Chief, will not run from the battle. Not when my prestige is at stake! If I have to call in air strikes over the playgrounds, I will do it! Let's see them try to bring down B-52's with their bats and their balls! Let's see them try to flee from my helicopters on those little tricycles of theirs! No, this mighty giant of a nation of which I am, by extension, the mighty giant of a

President, will not have its nose tweaked by a bunch of little brats who should be at home with their homework in the first place!

(*All applaud*)

Now, as to the voting. Since I am a decisive man, as you can see from my book *Six Hundred Crises,* I am now going to decide how many of these five enemies of America each of you will be allowed to choose to charge with the crime. Of course, we still have to decide which of the three crimes that the Professor mentioned we're going to use, but in that it is getting on to morning, perhaps we can put that off to a later date. In the meantime, we will come to a decision as to *who* is guilty. (*Impish endearing smile*) That's the best part, anyway!

Now (*back to serious business*), we will proceed in the following manner: the Professor will read his list, and each person present will select as many as he wants, up to three … No, two … No, three … Uh-oh, my lip's sweating—uh-oh, I think I'm having another crisis! *Two! Two! Say two!*

POLITICAL COACH: Good going, Mr. President—you've weathered it!

TRICKY: Wow! That makes six hundred and *two* crises! Wait'll I tell the girls what Daddy did!

LEGAL COACH: Mr. President, in that we are to be allowed only two of the candidates from the Professor's list, may I ask if we can each add two names of our own, should we think we have two more that warrant suspicion?

TRICKY: Well, let *me* ask *you* a question. Is this a deal you want to make?

LEGAL COACH: Well, if you want to think of it that way, that's okay with me.

TRICKY: I'd prefer to. Otherwise it might seem that I was changing my mind because I'm indecisive. But if it's just a matter of a payoff for something or other you'll deliver in the future, I think everybody here will understand.

LEGAL COACH: Suits me.

TRICKY: There we are then. Two from the Professor's list and two of your own choice.

HIGHBROW COACH: To the list then, gentlemen. 1: Hanoi.

2: The Berrigans. 3: The Black Panthers. 4: Jane Fonda. 5:
Curt Flood.

ALL: *Curt Flood?*

HIGHBROW COACH: Curt ... Flood.

SPIRITUAL COACH: But—isn't he a *baseball* player?

TRICKY: *Was* a baseball player. Any questions about baseball players, just ask me, Reverend. *Was* the center fielder for
the Washington Senators. But then he up and ran away.
Skipped the country.

HIGHBROW COACH: He did indeed, Mr. President. Curt
Flood, born January 18, 1938, in Houston, Texas, bats right,
throws right, entered big league baseball in 1956 with Cincin-
nati, played from '58 to '69 with the St. Louis Cardinals,
presently under contract at a salary of $110,000 a year to the
Washington Senators, on the morning of April 27, 1971, with
the baseball season not even a month old, boarded a Pan Am
flight bound from New York to Barcelona, giving no explanation for his hasty departure other than 'personal problems.'
Though Flood is known to have purchased a ticket for Barcelona, he apparently disembarked in Lisbon—wearing a brown
leather jacket, bell-bottomed trousers and sunglasses—there to
make connections with a flight for his final European destina-
tion ... The question, gentlemen, is obvious: why, a week to
the day before the uprising of the Boy Scouts in Washington,
D.C., why did Mr. Curt Flood of the Washington baseball
team find it necessary to leave the country in so precipitous
and dramatic a fashion?

TRICKY: Oh, I think I can answer that one, Professor,
knowing sports as I do inside and out. Poor Flood was in a
slump, and a bad one. In his first twenty times at bat this year,
he'd had only three hits, and two of those were bunts. Fact is,
Williams had benched him. He'd sat out six starts in a row
against right-hand pitching. Now I may be the highest
elected official in the land, but I still don't think I'm going to
second-guess Ted Williams when he benches a hitter. No,
sirree. On the other hand, you can well imagine the effect
being benched had upon a one-hundred-thousand-dollar-a-
year star player like Flood.

47

HIGHBROW COACH: With all due respect, sir, for your knowledge of the game, which far exceeds my own, this 'slump,' as you call it, might it not have been just the right 'cover' for a baseball player planning to leave the country in a hurry, just the right alibi?

LEGAL COACH: If I get your drift, Professor, are you suggesting that Ted Williams, the manager of the Senators, is implicated in this as well? That benching Flood was part of some overall plan?

POLITICAL COACH: Now hold on. Before we carry this any further, I want to say that I think we are skating on very thin ice here, when we are dealing with a baseball figure of Ted Williams' stature. Despised as he was by many sportswriters in his time—and I'm sure we could call upon these people for assistance, if we should want them—my gut reaction is that it is in the best interests of this administration to maintain a hands-off policy on all Hall of Famers.

TRICKY: And *what* a Hall of Famer! I wonder how many of you know Ted Williams' record. It certainly is a record for all Americans to be proud of, and I'd like to share it with you. Just listen and tell me if you don't agree. Lifetime batting average, .344. That makes him *fifth* in the history of the game. Lifetime slugging average, .634. *That* makes him second only to Babe Ruth himself! In doubles, fourteenth with 525; in home runs fifth with 521; in extra base hits seventh with 1,117; and in all-important RBI's, and I really can't say enough about RBI's and how important they are to the national pastime, in RBI's, also seventh with 1,839. And that isn't all. Led the league in hitting in 1941 with an average of—just listen to this—.406! In '42 again, with .356; in '47 with .343; in '48 with .369—(*Suddenly angry*) And they said Jack Charisma was the one who had the memory for facts! They said *Charisma* was the one who had the grasp of the issues! Oh, how they loved to downgrade Dixon! No wonder I had a crisis in that campaign! They were always picking on me! My beard! My nose! My tactics! Well, just let me say one thing as regards my so-called 'tactics': if in any of the averages I have just quoted to you, I have altered Ted Wil-

We love life

When you've got time really to enjoy life you need the money to do so.

£10,000 when you retire

by taking out now a Prudential Endowment Assurance. For more details, complete and return this card.

Some examples

The value of Prudential policies has been amply demonstrated over the years, as is shown by these examples of payments on claims under Ordinary Branch with-profits endowment assurances for £5,000 taken out in the U.K., and which matured at age 65 on 1st April, 1971.

Age at entry	30	40	50
Sum assured	£5,000	£5,000	£5,000
Bonuses*	£6,445	£5,155	£3,370
	£11,445	£10,155	£8,370

*Bonuses on future maturities cannot be guaranteed

CN/11/71/1158/FP(1460)

DO NOT AFFIX POSTAGE STAMPS IF POSTED IN
GT. BRITAIN, CHANNEL ISLANDS OR N. IRELAND

BUSINESS REPLY SERVICE
LICENCE No. K.E. 1511

The Chief General Manager
THE PRUDENTIAL ASSURANCE CO. LTD.

142 HOLBORN BARS
LONDON EC1N 2NH

POSTAGE WILL
BE PAID BY
LICENSEE

liams' record by so much as one hundredth of one percentage point, I will submit my resignation to Congress tomorrow. Now that would be an unprecedented act in American history, but I would do it, if I had dared to play party politics with the American public on a matter as serious as this one.

(*All applaud*)

POLITICAL COACH: Mr. President, that was a most impressive recitation of the facts, and has only served to strengthen my conviction that it would be utterly foolhardy to bring a slugger like Williams under federal indictment.

TRICKY: Good thinking. Good sharp political thinking. Of course, with Flood himself, we have a very different situation. To be sure, he batted over .300 for the Cards in '61, '63, '64, '65, '67 and '68, but never once did he lead the league in hitting or home runs, as Williams did, and his slugging average is almost *half* what Williams' was at the end of his career.

Of course, in 1964, Flood *did* lead the National League in base hits with 211, and something like that could stir up a certain amount of sympathy. Now let me make one thing perfectly clear: I am not saying that he is anywhere near the all-time leader in that department, George Sisler, who got 257 hits in the year 1920, but a fact is a fact, and we are going to have to confront it. Those 211 base hits could mean trouble.

HIGHBROW COACH: Mr. President, under ordinary circumstances I too might be leery of bringing a charge as drastic as whichever one we come up with, against a man who, as you so wisely remind us, led the National League in total base hits with 211. But Curt Flood is something more than your run-of-the-mill hitting star of yesteryear; he is a bona fide troublemaker, and was in hot water right up to his neck even before I put him on my list. That is *why* I put him on my list: for not only has he jumped a hundred-thousand-dollar contract and skipped the country only a month into the season, but he of course is the man who in 1970 refused to be traded by the St. Louis Cardinals to the Philadelphia Phillies, claiming that the trade denied him his basic rights to negotiate a contract for his services on the open market. Subsequently, he hired as his attorney none other than Lyin' B. Johnson's appointee to the

Supreme Court ...

POLITICAL COACH (*hopefully*): Abe Fortas!

HIGHBROW COACH: No, no, but almost as good. Arthur Goldberg. G-o-l-d-b-e-r-g. And these two instituted a suit against baseball on constitutional grounds, asserting that organized baseball was in violation of the Antitrust Laws, and that the owners, by trading players from one team to another without their permission, treated them like pieces of property, which was both illegal and immoral.

Now, impugning the sacred name of baseball in this way did not go over very well with a good many loyal Americans, including the Commissioner of Baseball himself, and in the eyes of many, sportswriters and fellow players, as well as fans throughout the country, Flood, and his mouthpiece Goldberg, appeared to be out to destroy the game beloved by millions. Flood, in a book he has written on the subject, even quotes himself as saying in conversation, 'Somebody needs to go up against the system. I'm ready.' And, gentlemen, that is only *one* of the self-incriminating statements that is scattered throughout that manifesto. Of course, as if all that he has said and done isn't compromising enough—including hiring a Mr. *Goldberg* to represent him in this attack upon the most American of American sports—Flood is a black man.

LEGAL COACH: Where is he now, Algeria? That would sew it up for us, if he was in Algeria.

HIGHBROW COACH: To the contrary, had he fled to Algeria —which he has not—they would already be selling posters of him at bat in a beret, and ads to 'Free Flood' would be appearing daily in *The New York Times*, signed by movie stars and Jean-Paul Sartre. There'd be marches and pickets and probably one of those mule trains camping on the White House lawn.

TRICKY: Oh, those mule trains! Those marches! Really, I can't *stand* those things. It never fails—every time they start marching on Washington, *I'm* the one who has to leave town. Now does that make any sense to you? *I'm* the President, I *live* here, and still *I'm* the one who has to pack his bags and get on a helicopter and go when these marchers start pouring in from all over the country! Honestly, I've got this big beautiful house, and I spend half my life living out of suitcases. Can you imagine what it's like for a President, on practically five minutes' notice, to try to pack everything he needs in his briefcase, while outside the window the propellers are going and everybody is screaming 'Hurry, hurry, let's get out of here, before they go crazy and send a delegation to the door!' Oh, it's just awful. One time I forgot my jersey, one time I forgot my cleats, one time I even forgot to pack my ball—and really, the whole weekend was just *ruined*. And those marchers couldn't care less!

HIGHBROW COACH: Well, you won't have to leave town this time, Mr. President. Because this fugitive has not fled to Algeria to set himself up as some kind of ersatz revolutionary leader in exile; nor has he fled to Africa to live among his own kind, as he might have done if he were looking to build a following. No, there isn't going to be much sympathy in this country, I can assure you, for a handsome and muscular young black man like Mr. Curt Flood, who, from all indications, has decided to make his home—gentlemen, it couldn't be better—in Copenhagen.

SPIRITUAL COACH: *No!*

HIGHBROW COACH: Yes, Reverend, Copenhagen. The Mecca toward which the filth peddlers of the world go down on their knees morning and night. The pornography capital of the world.

POLITICAL COACH: Wow! (*Ecstatic*) And that's not all they've got in Denmark to compromise Mr. Flood, is it?

HIGHBROW COACH: Very fast on your feet, young man ... The word is miscegenation. Not that we have to come right out with it, any more than we mean to say, in so many words, that he is a known smut addict.

SPIRITUAL COACH: No, please, you mustn't. Where a baseball star is involved, we are inevitably going to be dealing with young impressionable minds, boys eight, nine, ten years of age—— If they were to hear such words ...

POLITICAL COACH: I agree, Reverend. It'll be better by far to do it by 'implication.'

LEGAL COACH: Fine with me. What about you, Mr. President? Think you can manage that? A hint here, a slur there, instead of coming right out with it?

TRICKY: Well, if it's a matter of making the Reverend feel at ease about the wonderful young Little Leaguers of this country, I sure am going to try.

SPIRITUAL COACH: Thank you, Mr. President. Thank you, gentlemen.

TRICKY: You see, Reverend, there's that restraint again, there's that sense of proportion and moderation that according to the newspapers I'm not supposed to have. After all, here is a black man engaging in just about the wickedest act any American can imagine, and with the women of Denmark, who are among the whitest in the entire world, and yet instead of coming right out with it, and thus exposing our Little Leaguers to a highly dangerous and tempting idea, we are going to smear him by insinuation and innuendo.

SPIRITUAL COACH: I'm deeply indebted, Mr. President.

POLITICAL COACH: We thought that went without saying, Reverend.

HIGHBROW COACH: Good enough, gentlemen. I shall now proceed to read the list one more time, so that you may decide how you wish to cast your votes. 1: Hanoi. 2: The Berrigans——

POLITICAL COACH: May I interrupt here? I wonder if I can take a moment to make a case for the innocence of the Berrigan brothers.

LEGAL COACH (*outraged*): The *innocence* of the *Berrigan brothers*?

POLITICAL COACH (*backpeddling*): Of this charge! Of this charge!

LEGAL COACH: But we haven't even decided yet upon the exact *nature* of the charge—so how can they be innocent? Where is your evidence? Where is your proof?

POLITICAL COACH: Well, I don't have any.

LEGAL COACH: Then, maybe, young man, you oughtn't to go around calling people innocent until you do!

POLITICAL COACH: I *grant* you that—but what I am fearful

of is this: if we do try to pin still another crime on those priests, we are going to produce a sympathetic reaction toward them such as you ordinarily don't get until after an assassination. I should tell you that at this very moment a Hollywood movie is in the early stages of planning, in which Fathers Phil and Dan Berrigan are to be portrayed by Bing Crosby and an actor, as yet unnamed, who will be made up to resemble the late, great Barry Fitzgerald. Now these Hollywood producers, gentlemen, no matter how they may dress or wear their hair, are not hippies or left-wing fanatics by any stretch of the imagination. Underneath those anti-establishment mutton-chops they are hard-headed businessmen with a product to market and an audience to exploit, and they can spot a trend developing a long way off. According to my informants, the movie being planned deals sympathetically with two priests who decide to blow up West Point, after Army defeats Notre Dame before seventy million television fans in the big football game of the year. There'll be nuns and songs and so on, and who knows but that a picture like this could turn the whole damn country Communist overnight.

MILITARY COACH: Two hundred million Reds on American soil? Not if I have anything to say about it.

POLITICAL COACH: Easier said than done, General. Shoot two hundred million Americans—if that's what you have in mind—shoot *one* hundred million Americans, and I'm afraid you're going to give the Democrats just the kind of issue they can play politics with in the '72 elections.

MILITARY COACH: The level to which political life in this country has sunk! Now if the military were running this show...

POLITICAL COACH: Granted. Granted. But you do not build a utopian society overnight, General. And that is why I wish to caution you, one and all, against voting for the Berrigans. I know how tempting it is, especially after what we went through to track them down, but I am afraid that this is another one of those instances when we are going to have to display our characteristic restraint and moderation. Certainly the last thing in the world we want is Bing Crosby in a collar

53

crooning to Debbie Reynolds in her habit about b-b-b-b-lowing things up. Not even Lenin could have devised a more sure-fire method of converting the American working class into bomb-throwing revolutionaries.

HIGHBROW COACH: Ingenious analysis. Nonetheless, I think you misread Hollywood's intentions. If the Berrigans were to get the chair, to be sure Hollywood would immediately go into full-scale production of some kind of musical about them, along the line of *Going My Way*. But that is only an argument against killing them. Keep them in jail, and you will be surprised how quickly the public *and* the movie moguls will forget they exist.

LEGAL COACH: I agree. Bury them alive. Always better.

SPIRITUAL COACH: And more merciful, too. That way, you see, it's not capital punishment.

HIGHBROW COACH: To move on then. Number two was the Berrigans.

SPIRITUAL COACH: What was one again? Harvard?

HIGHBROW COACH: Hanoi.

SPIRITUAL COACH: Ah, yes. I knew it was something beginning with an H.

MILITARY COACH (*angrily*): And what about something *else* beginning with an 'H'? What about Haiphong! How can you have Hanoi without Haiphong? That's like Quemoy without Matsu!

TRICKY: Quemoy and Matsu! Does *that* bring back memories! Quemoy and Matsu! ... What ever happened to them?

POLITICAL COACH: Oh, they're still out there, Mr. President, if we should ever need them.

TRICKY: Well, that's wonderful. Where were they again—exactly? Wait, let me guess, let's see if I can remember ... Indonesia!

POLITICAL COACH: No, sir.

TRICKY: Am I warm? The Philippines! No? ... Near Hawaii? ... No? Oh, I give up.

POLITICAL COACH: In the Formosa Straits, Mr. President. Between Taiwan and Mainland China.

TRICKY: No kidding. Hey, listen, whatever happened to what's-his-name? The Chinaman.

POLITICAL COACH: Which Chinaman, Mr. President? There are six hundred million Chinamen.

TRICKY: I know, enslaved and so on. But I'm thinking of, you know, the one with the wife. Oh, it's one of those names they have ...

HIGHBROW COACH: Chiang Kai-shek, Mr. President.

TRICKY: Right, Professor! Shek. Little Shek, with the glasses. (*Fondly*) The Old Dixon ... (*Chuckling*) Well! Enough wandering down memory lane. Forgive me, gentlemen. Where were we? So far we have Moscow and the Berrigans.

HIGHBROW COACH: Hanoi and the Berrigans, Mr. President.

TRICKY: Of course! See what you did with that Quemoy and Matsu? I was still back there in the fifties. Look at me, my lip is covered with goose flesh.

HIGHBROW COACH: To proceed. Number 3: The Black Panthers. No dispute there. Good. Number 4: Jane Fonda, the movie actress and antiwar activist. Number 5: Curt Flood, the baseball player. Any questions, before we proceed to the vote. Reverend?

SPIRITUAL COACH: Jane Fonda. Has she ever appeared nude in a film?

HIGHBROW COACH: I can't honestly say I remember seeing her pudenda on the screen, Reverend, but I think I can vouch for her breasts.

SPIRITUAL COACH: With aureole or without?

HIGHBROW COACH: I believe with.

SPIRITUAL COACH: And her buttocks?

HIGHBROW COACH: Yes, I believe we've seen her buttocks. Indeed, they constitute a large part of her appeal.

SPIRITUAL COACH: Thank you.

HIGHBROW COACH: Any other questions?

POLITICAL COACH: Well, about the Black Panthers—do you really think that the American people will believe that the Black Panthers are behind *the Boy Scouts*? That really does require quite a bit of imagination.

TRICKY: Now I take exception there. I don't want to influence the voting, but I do want to say this: let's not underestimate the imagination of the American people. This may seem like old-fashioned patriotism such as isn't in fashion any more, but I have the highest regard for their imagination and I always have. Why, I actually think the American people can be made to believe anything. These people, after all, have their fantasies and fears and superstitions, just like anybody else, and you are not going to put anything over on them by simply addressing yourself to the real problems and pretending that the others don't exist just because they are imaginary.

HIGHBROW COACH: I agree wholeheartedly, Mr. President. May we proceed to the voting?

TRICKY: By all means ... Of course, gentlemen, these *are* going to be free elections. I want it to be perfectly clear beforehand that I wouldn't have it otherwise, unless there were some reason to believe that the vote might go the wrong way. And I am proud to say I don't think that's possible here in this locker room with men of your caliber. You may vote for any two candidates on the list, and you may, in the interest of justice, add any two names of your own choosing. I will write down the votes cast for each candidate and tabulate them on this sheet of paper.

Now you'll see that this is an ordinary sheet of lined yellow paper such as you might find on any legal pad. I was a lawyer, you know, before I became President, so you can be pretty sure that I know the correct manner in which to use this kind of paper. In fact, I should like you now to examine the paper to be sure nothing has been written on it and that it contains no code markings or secret notations other than the usual watermark.

HIGHBROW COACH: I'm sure we all can trust your description of the piece of paper, Mr. President.

TRICKY: I appreciate your confidence, Professor, but I would still prefer that the four of you examine the paper thoroughly beforehand, so that afterwards there cannot be any doubt as to the one hundred percent honesty of this electoral procedure. (*He hands the paper around to each*) Good! Now for a free election! Suppose we begin with you, Reverend.

SPIRITUAL COACH: Well, really, I'm in a tizzy. I mean, I know for sure that I want to vote for Jane Fonda—but after her I just can't make up my mind. Curt Flood is *so* tempting.

HIGHBROW COACH: Vote for both then.

TRICKY: Or suppose you think it through a little longer and we'll come back to you. General?

MILITARY COACH (*belligerently*): Hanoi and Haiphong!

TRICKY: In other words, that's your write-in vote, Haiphong.

MILITARY COACH: Mine, and every loyal American's, Mr. President!

TRICKY: Fair enough. (*Records vote*) Next.

POLITICAL COACH: I'll take Hanoi, too.

TRICKY: With or without Haiphong?

POLITICAL COACH: I think I like it just by itself.

TRICKY: And, anything else?

POLITICAL COACH: No, thank you, Mr. President—I stick.

TRICKY: Okay, time to hear the voice of Justice.

LEGAL COACH: The Berrigans, the Panthers, Curt Flood.

TRICKY: Slowly, please, slowly. I want to be sure to get it right. The Berrigans ... The Panthers ... Curt Flood ... But that's three. You're allowed only two.

LEGAL COACH: I understand that, Mr. President. But in that my predecessors have each used only one from the Professor's list of five, it did not seem to me a violation of the *spirit* of the law, if I took up some of the slack. I am a great believer, as I think you are, sir, in the spirit of the law, if not the letter.

TRICKY: Well, okay, if that's the reason. Do you want now to add any names of your own?

LEGAL COACH: As a matter of fact, Mr. President, I do.

TRICKY: One or two?

LEGAL COACH: As a matter of fact, Mr. President, five.

TRICKY: *Five?* But you were the one who made up the rule about only *two.*

LEGAL COACH: And I stand by it, Mr. President, or would,

under the circumstances such as existed at the time I suggested it. But I am dealing at this moment with what I can only call 'a clear and present danger.' I am afraid, Mr. President, that if I were to submit only two of these five names that I have just this minute come up with, this administration would be in the most serious clear and present danger you can imagine of appearing to be out of its mind. If, on the other hand, the five names are submitted together, thus suggesting some kind of plot, a charge that might otherwise have appeared, at best, to be an opportunistic and vicious attack on two individuals we don't happen to like, will take on an air of the plausible in the mind of the nation, such as it is.

Surely, Mr. President, you will permit me at least to *read* the names of the five. This is, after all, a free country where even the man in the street can say what's on his mind, provided it isn't so provocative that it might lead somebody in another state, who doesn't even hear it, to riot. It would be a sad irony indeed, if the man who is this nation's bulwark against those very riots that such freedom of speech tends to inspire, was to be denied *his* rights under the First Amendment.

TRICKY: It would, it would. And you can rest assured that so long as I am President that particular sad irony—if I understand it correctly—is not going to happen.

LEGAL COACH: Thank you, Mr. President. Now try not to think of the five individually, but rather as a kind of secret gang, protected, as much as anything, by the seeming disparateness of individual personality and profession. 1: the folk singer, Joan Baez. 2: the Mayor of New York, John Lancelot. 3: the dead rock musician, Jimi Hendrix. 4: the TV star, Johnny Carson...

ALL: *Johnny Carson?*

LEGAL COACH (*smiling*): Who better to be acquitted? It's always best, you see, to have one acquitted, especially if he appears to have been unjustly accused in the first place. It provides the jury with a means of funneling all their uncertainty in one direction, makes them feel they've been fair about the whole thing. Makes the convictions themselves look better all around. And, of course, freeing Johnny Carson, you'll be freeing the most popular man in America (besides yourself, Mr. President). Why, we can even, midway through the trial, have the President step in and make a statement in Carson's behalf. Exactly as he did about Manson, only the other way around this time. Imagine, the whole country crying 'Free Johnny!' and the President going on TV and casting serious doubt on the charges raised against this great entertainer.

TRICKY: And then when he's free, I could have a press conference! Wouldn't that be something? I could say, '*H-e-e-e-re's* Johnny,' and he could come out from behind the curtain and do his cute little golf stroke! He could make jokes about being in jail with the other conspirators. Maybe he could even wear a ball and chain and a striped suit!

POLITICAL COACH: Fantastic! And we could do it on prime time the night before the election. While Musty is boring their pants off about how honest the pine trees are in Maine, we'll be on TV with Johnny Carson!

LEGAL COACH: And that's not all, gentlemen. You have not yet heard the name of the *fifth* conspirator.

POLITICAL COACH: Merv Griffin!

LEGAL COACH: No, not Merv Griffin ... Jacqueline Charisma Colossus.

(*Stunned silence*)

Daring, yes. Absurd? I think not. Consider first, gentlemen, that like the other four conspirators, her Christian name too begins with a 'J'. Now you cannot imagine the mileage we can get out of a seemingly nonsensical fact like that. Overnight the newspapers and the TV commentators are going to begin calling them 'The Five J's,' thereby linking them together in the public mind as though they were the Dionne quintuplets, or the New York Knicks. Just by that ruse alone, we will have moved halfway toward a conviction. Inevitably there will be speculation—we'll see to that—about the relationship between Mrs. Colossus and Mayor Lancelot. Isn't it about time that we turned those looks of his to our advantage instead of his? Then too there is the former First Lady's bitterness toward her own

59

country, as manifested in her decision to marry a foreigner and live in a foreign country.

POLITICAL COACH: Well, it isn't exactly as though she's living in Peking or Hanoi, you know.

LEGAL COACH: I've considered that, and I think that the wisest course to follow is not to mention the name of the country itself. We'll just keep saying foreign—suggesting intrigue and despots and shady operations—and hope that nobody will remember it's only Greece.

POLITICAL COACH: Jackie and Lancelot—I've got to admit, we're going to get the headlines on this one. But why Jimi Hendrix, if he's dead?

LEGAL COACH: Because we haven't had a rock performer yet. And personally I think the parents of the country are ready to hang one of those bastards. We'll start cautiously, however, with a dead one. And if we don't pick up any flak there, we'll get ourselves a live one in time for the election ... And, of course, last but not least, his name begins with a 'J.'

TRICKY: I must say, from the sound of it, you certainly appear to have thought this through in all its ramifications in only about five minutes. The political advantages to be gained by associating Lancelot and the Charisma name with rock singers and folk singers seem to me inestimable. And indicting and then freeing Johnny Carson is probably just about the most fantastic opportunity for self-aggrandizement I've come upon since Hiss.

LEGAL COACH: Thank you, Mr. President.

TRICKY: But—and this is a very big but—there is the rule, of your own devising, that we all agreed to earlier. Yes, I know you see this as 'a clear and present danger' to the party—but I happen to see it as nothing short of a tremendous boon. Consequently, I am not going to allow you to submit these five names. But—and here is an even bigger but—*but*, because the five *are* inextricably linked by their first initial, I am going to ask you rather to submit them as though they were one. And to indicate that they are to be tabulated as one and not five, I am going to place a large bracket here in the margin, like so ... See? I want all of you to see. I have just done exactly as I said

I would. Please take a good long look, so that afterwards there is no cause to question the honesty of these proceedings. (*All examine the bracket and agree it is a bracket, just as the President said*) Now then, Professor. Your vote.

HIGHBROW COACH: I cast my vote for Curt Flood and Curt Flood alone. Not only is his a fresh name to a country that is growing pretty weary of the Berrigans and the Panthers—and, with all due respect, is sick to death of Jacqueline Charisma— but on top of that he is, as I said earlier, someone we can slander and vilify without any danger of turning him into a hero or a martyr. In the argot of baseball, he is a natural.

TRICKY: Very good. (*Records the vote*) And, Reverend? Have you reached a final decision? You can't say I haven't given you time to make a wise choice.

SPIRITUAL COACH: No, I can't. Only I'm afraid that having listened to everything that's been said, I'm really more confused now than when I began. I mean I'm still very much for Jane Fonda. She is still far and away my first choice. But once I get beyond her—well, I just can't make up my mind. And it really would be terrible to do the wrong thing, wouldn't it, given the gravity and seriousness of what we're about . . .? (*To the General*) Excuse me, but who did you vote for again?

MILITARY COACH: Hanoi and Haiphong.

SPIRITUAL COACH (*to Political Coach*): And you?

POLITICAL COACH: Hanoi, without Haiphong.

SPIRITUAL COACH (*to Legal Coach*): And you have the five-in-one—and what were the others?

LEGAL COACH: Berrigans, Panthers and Flood.

SPIRITUAL COACH (*throwing his hands up*): Oh, this is just impossible! Each one sounds better than the one before! Oh—the heck with it! Eeny, meeny, miney, moe . . . Okay! Jane Fonda *and* Curt Flood! Done!

TRICKY: (*Records the Reverend's vote*) Now that all the ballots have been cast, gentlemen, I am going once again to pass this sheet of paper among you so that you may be certain that your votes have been correctly tabulated. Even the President of the United States, you know, is capable of making a clerical error, and if he has, he certainly hopes that he can be a big enough man to admit it. (*He passes the paper among them*)

LEGAL COACH: Jimi Hendrix, Mr. President—the first name is spelled J-i-m-i, not J-i-m-m-y, as you've written it here.

TRICKY: Well, let's correct it then, because that is just the sort of error, inadvertently made, that tends to be totally misconstrued by the press. Now I never claimed to know how to spell the names of every colored person in this country, but I will tell you this much: where someone's name is concerned, colored or not, he has a constitutional right to have it spelled correctly on any indictment that is handed down on him, no matter how absurd or outrageous the charges themselves. And so long as I am President, I am going to make every effort to see that this is done. Now, J-i-m *what*?

LEGAL COACH: I.

TRICKY: J-i-m-*i*. There. And I'll initial the change, just to make clear exactly who is responsible for both the error and the correction. There!

Now I only wish that the wonderful colored people of this country could have seen the scrupulosity with which I attended to a matter seemingly so picayune as this one. Oh sure, the media would still find something to carp about, you can bank on that. But I am certain, if I know the great majority of good, hard-working colored people in this country, that the time I just took from my pressing duties as President of the United States and Leader of the Free World to correct a single letter in one of their names would not have gone unnoticed and unappreciated. Call me a dreamer; call me a believer in humanity; call me, as the song has it, a cockeyed optimist; and be sure to call me a big man too, for admitting to my error; but I am sure that they would understand just how difficult a problem this is for us to solve, given the kinds of ways they spell those names of theirs, and I think they would have that wonderful wisdom, such as comes to people who work in menial occupations, to realize that a job of these proportions is not going to be completed overnight, and that consequently we are not about to be bullied into spelling their names correctly by marches or demonstrations or mule trains parked on the

White House lawn. We will spell them right but in our own sweet time, and according to our own secret timetable, on earth as it is in Heaven.

SPIRITUAL COACH: Amen.

TRICKY: And, my friends, on that sanctimonious note, I am going to call this conference to a close. At ten A.M., we shall meet to settle upon the exact nature of the crime. In the meantime, I will remain here in the locker room, in uniform...

SPIRITUAL COACH: Mr. President, it is nearly dawn. You must get some rest. You must take your helmet off and go to bed.

TRICKY: I couldn't sleep now, Reverend, if I tried. Not with a smear campaign of this magnitude before me.

SPIRITUAL COACH: But a man has only so much to give...

TRICKY: When it comes to something like this, Reverend, I have to say, immodest as it may sound, I am indefatigable. No, I will remain in uniform, helmet and all, and with the aid of the ballots you have cast here in this free election, I will hammer out, in the lonely vigil of the night, the conspiracy that seems to me most beneficial to my career. I only hope and pray that I am equal to the task. Good night, gentlemen, and thank you.

ALL: Good night, Mr. President. (*They rise to leave*)

TRICKY: And don't forget to hand in your uniforms at the door. I won't mention names, but I understand that last time one of you tried to smuggle his out, under his street clothes, in order to show off at home to his wife and children. Of course, I understand the temptation. How many times have I wanted to address the nation in my shoulder guards! I've never told this to a soul, but strictly between us, at the time of the Cambodian incursion, I did go on nationwide TV, unbeknownst to everyone, wearing my regulation National Football League athletic supporter. I just couldn't help myself. I'd seen *Patton* and I'd invaded Cambodia, and I guess the whole thing went to my head. Of course, not a word beyond these four walls: if any of my critics found out, well, you know how they like to jump on Dixon. All I have to do is wear a football player's jockstrap on TV while making a foreign policy speech and the morning papers would have me pegged as a psychopath. Down here in the secret underground locker room, it's one thing—up there in the real world, banker's gray!

ALL: You can trust us with your secrets, Mr. President.

TRICKY (*moved*): I know I can ... All right, then. It remains only for each of you, as he passes from the room, to slap me on the behind the way the pros do coming out of the huddle. And don't forget to say, 'Way to go, Tricky D, way to go!'

FOUR

TRICKY ADDRESSES
THE NATION

*(The Famous 'Something is Rotten in
the State of Denmark' Speech)*

Good evening, my fellow Americans.

I come before you tonight with a message of national importance. While it is true that I do not intend to offer you false hope by minimizing the nature of the crisis confronting our nation at this hour, I do not believe there is cause for any such alarm as you may have seen or heard in the news media from those critical of the decisions I have reached in the last twenty-four hours.

Now I know there are always those who would prefer that we take a weak, cowardly and dishonorable position in the face of a crisis. They of course are entitled to their opinion. I am certain, however, that the great majority of the American people will agree that the actions I have taken in the confrontation between the United States of America and the sovereign state of Denmark are indispensable to our dignity, our honor, our moral and spiritual idealism, our credibility around the world, the soundness of the economy, our greatness, our dedication to the vision of our forefathers, the human spirit, the divinely inspired dignity of man, our treaty commitments, the principles of the United Nations and progress and peace for all people.

Now no one is more aware than I am of the political consequences of taking bold and forthright action in behalf of our dignity, idealism and honor, to choose just three. But I would rather be a one-term President and take these noble, heroic measures against the state of Denmark, than be a two-term President by accepting humiliation at the hands of a tenth-rate military power. I want to make that perfectly clear.

Let me tell you now the measures I have ordered taken to deal with Denmark, and the reasons for my decision. (*Picks up his pointer and turns to map of Scandinavia*)

First: Despite the treacherous manner in which the Pro-Pornography government in Copenhagen has moved against the United States, I have responded swiftly and effectively to gain the military initiative. At this very moment, the American Sixth Fleet, dispatched by my order to the Baltic and the North Seas, is in complete command of the waterways to and from Denmark, as indicated on this map. (*Points to the Baltic Sea and the North Sea*) Aircraft carriers, troop ships and destroyers have been placed in a strategic ring around the Danish peninsula of Jutland (*points*) and the numerous adjacent Danish islands, all of which you see here colored in red. Taken together these territories make Denmark approximately as large (*turns to map of United States*) as the wonderful states of New Hampshire and Vermont, famous for their beautiful autumn foliage and delicious maple syrup, and colored here in white.

Now let me tell you the results of this action, ordered by me as Commander-in-Chief of the Armed Forces meeting his responsibilities.

To all intents and purposes, Denmark is at this time isolated by a blockade as impenetrable as the blockade with which President John F. Charisma in 1962 prevented Soviet nuclear missiles from entering Cuba and the Western Hemisphere, which is here (*points to map of Western Hemisphere*). And that as we all know was the finest and most courageous hour of his Presidency. This blockade, then, is exactly like that one.

Now while it is true that I have effectively isolated Denmark from the rest of the world, I have refused to take an isolationist position for America of the kind my critics would counsel me to take in this crisis. Because let there be no mistake about it: America cannot live in isolation if it expects to live in peace.

Now I hear you ask: 'Mr. President, you have moved swiftly and effectively to protect our dignity, idealism and honor; but what about our national security—isn't that endangered, too?'

Well, that is a good question and one that deserves a thoughtful answer. For we are all familiar with the belligerent and expansionist policies of the state of Denmark, in particular the territorial designs that country has had upon the continental United States ever since the eleventh century. As you remember, at that time landings were made upon the North American continent by forces under the command of Eric the Red, and later under the command of his son, Leif Ericson. These landings by the Red family and their Viking hordes were of course made without warning and in direct violation of the Monroe Doctrine. Aside from these invasions of a paramilitary nature, there were also various unsuccessful attempts made by these Vikings to establish privileged sanctuaries on our eastern seaboard, right here (*points*) in the vicinity of Boston, the birthplace of Paul Revere and his world-renowned midnight ride, and the site of the famous Boston Tea Party.

So when you ask me if our national security is threatened by these Danes, with their long-standing history of open contempt for our territorial integrity, I think I have to answer in all candor, yes it is. And that is why I have made clear to the Pro-Pornography government in Copenhagen tonight that I do not intend to react to any renewed threat to our territorial integrity, to our honor or to our idealism, with plaintive diplomatic protests. And in order that there should be no misunderstanding of my position, I have ordered the American Seventh Army, stationed in West Germany, to be mobilized in striking position here (*points*) at the fifty-fifth parallel on the border between Germany and Denmark. And I assure you, my fellow Americans, as I have assured the Pro-Pornography government in Copenhagen, and as I would have assured the Red family regime in the eleventh century had I been your President at that time, that I will not for a moment hesitate to send our brave American fighting men over the border and into

Denmark tonight, if that is what is necessary to prevent our children from having to fight the descendants of Eric the Red in the streets of (*pointing with his pointer*) Portland, Boston, New York, Philadelphia, Baltimore, Washington, Norfolk, Wilmington, Charleston, Savannah, Jacksonville, Miami, Key Biscayne and, of course, points west.

Now, though Denmark is effectively isolated from the world by the Sixth Fleet, and effectively threatened with occupation by the Seventh Army, the fact is that the Danish people have yet to see a single armed American soldier on their soil. Contrary to whatever wild rumors have been irresponsibly disseminated by the alarmists and sensationalists in the news media, the fact of the matter is that (*checks his watch*) as of this hour, we have no troops inside Denmark, serving either in a combat capacity, or as advisers in uniform to the Danish Anti-Pornography Resistance, considered by many the legitimate Danish government-in-exile.

Whatever reports you may have heard of an armed American invasion of Danish territory are categorically false, and constitute a deliberate distortion of the facts.

The truth is this: the amphibious landing by a detachment of one thousand brave American Marines that did occur only a few hours ago, at midnight Danish time, was not an invasion of Danish territory, but the liberation from Danish domination of a landmark that has been sacred for centuries to English-speaking peoples around the world, and particularly so to Americans.

I am speaking of the liberation of the town of Elsinore, the home of the fortress popularly known to tourists as 'Hamlet's Castle.' After centuries of occupation and touristic exploitation by the Danes, the town and the castle, which owe their fame entirely to William Shakespeare, the greatest writer of English in all recorded history, are occupied tonight by American soldiers, speaking the tongue of the immortal bard.

Let's look again at the map. Here on the coast is Elsinore, approximately thirty-five miles north of the capital city of Copenhagen. Because of its proximity to the capital, it was believed for centuries to be heavily guarded and impregnable to attack. It is surely a great tribute to both our intelligence units and our brave fighting Marines, that American forces were able to wade ashore at midnight and under cover of darkness drive the foreign invaders from the castle without firing a single shot.

I am proud to report that the guard on duty at Elsinore was so taken by surprise that when roused from his bed by a knocking at the gate, he came to the door in his pajamas and opened it so wide that our brave Marines were able to overrun and secure the grounds in a matter of minutes. The guard, who was the only foreign invader on the premises at that time, has been taken into custody, along with his tourist guidebooks, and a thorough interrogation is currently under way in the famous dungeons of the castle, in accordance with the rules laid down at the Geneva Convention, to which this country is a proud signatory.

Following the liberation of Elsinore, I have sent a communiqué to the Pro-Pornography government in Copenhagen, making it absolutely clear that our action was in no way directed to the security interests of any nation, Denmark included. Any government that chooses to use these actions as a pretext for harming relations with the United States will be doing so on its own responsibility, and we will draw the appropriate conclusions.

Incidentally, in that connection, if the Danish Army should attempt to harass or dislodge our Marines in any way whatsoever from 'Hamlet's Castle,' it would be interpreted by Americans of all walks of life, professors and poets as well as housewives and hardhats, as a direct affront to our national heritage. I would have no choice but to respond in kind by retaliating against the statue of Hans Christian Andersen in Copenhagen with the largest air strike ever called upon a European city.

I realize that as a result of my decision to free Elsinore from the yoke of foreign domination, the American people are going to be assailed by counsels of defeat and doubt from some of the most widely known opinion leaders of the nation. But let me say this to those defeatists and doubters: should the state of Denmark, now or in the future, attempt to occupy Mark Twain's Missouri, or the wonderful old South of *Gone with the Wind*, in the way that they have so ruthlessly occupied 'Hamlet's Castle' all these centuries, I would no more hesitate to send in the Marines to free Hannibal and Atlanta and Richmond and Jackson and St. Louis, than I did tonight to free Elsinore. And I firmly believe that the great majority of the American people would stand behind me then, as I know they do now.

Fortunately, however, I now have every expectation that not only our children, but our children's children, will never have to defend with their blood the literary landmarks of their native land from the onslaught of the Danish Tourist Office, because we, their parents, failed to do our duty by them in a quaint little seaside village in a faraway land.

The next move is up to Copenhagen. They have two choices. Either they can extend to us the diplomatic courtesy we have requested of them under international law; or, in the face of that request, they can continue to display the intransigence, belligerence and contempt that originally touched off this grave confrontation.

Now if they choose within the next twelve hours to negotiate with us in good faith by conceding to us what we want, I shall immediately call off the blockade of their coast, just as John F. Charisma called off the blockade of Cuba in his finest hour. Furthermore, I will reduce at the rate of one sixteenth a year the number of troops massed at their borders. Lastly, the guard taken prisoner at Elsinore castle will be returned to Copenhagen, provided the interrogation now being conducted does not reveal him to be a Danish citizen in the employ of the Danish government.

If, however, Copenhagen should refuse to negotiate in good faith by giving us what we want, I shall immediately order 100,000 armed American troops onto Danish soil.

Now, quickly, let me make one thing very clear: this will not constitute an invasion, either. Once we have overrun the country, bombarded the major cities, devastated the country-side, destroyed the military, disarmed the citizenry, jailed the

70

leaders of the Pro-Pornography government and established in Copenhagen the government currently in exile so that, as Abraham Lincoln said, it shall not perish from this earth, we shall immediately withdraw our troops.

For unlike the Danes, this great country harbors no designs on foreign territory. Nor do we wish to interfere in the internal affairs of another country. Despite our very deep sympathy with the aspirations of the Danish Anti-Pornography Resistance, we have over the years maintained a scrupulous wait-and-see attitude, in the hope that these eminently decent and idealistic men of the D.A.R. would be permitted to achieve political office in Copenhagen through democratic means. Unfortunately, the Pro-Pornography Party would not permit this to come about, but repeatedly, in one so-called free election after another, chose to brainwash the Danish people into voting *against* the D.A.R. So elaborate and thoroughgoing were these brainwashing techniques, that eventually the D.A.R. did not collect a single vote and, to all intents and purposes might just as well not have been on the ballot. In this way did the forces of filth and smut make a mockery of the democratic processes in Denmark.

My fellow Americans, it is precisely this sort of contempt for the rights of others that Copenhagen would now display toward the United States of America. Only this country is not about to be bullied and disgraced by a tenth-rate military power, and see our credibility destroyed in every area of the world where only the power of the United States deters aggression. And that is why tonight I have put the leaders in Copenhagen on notice that if they continue to refuse what we ask of them, I will bring all our military might to bear to restore to legitimate authority in Denmark a government that will respond to reason instead of force, a government that stands for decency instead of degradation, a government, as Abraham Lincoln said, of, by and for, not only the Danish people, but the American people and all good people everywhere.

What are we asking of Copenhagen, my fellow Americans? Neither more nor less than what we requested and received from the United Kingdom in 1968, when, according to the rules of international law and the custom of civilized nations, that country returned to our shores the fugitive from justice who was later convicted of the murder of Martin Luther King.

What are we asking of Copenhagen? Neither more nor less than what we would have requested of the Soviet Union in 1963, had President Charisma's murderer attempted to take refuge for a second time in that country.

What are we asking of Copenhagen? Nothing more nor less than that they surrender to the proper American authorities the fugitive from the Washington Senators of the American League of Professional Baseball Clubs, the man who fled this country on April 27, 1971, exactly one week to the day before the uprising of the Boy Scouts in Washington—the man named Charles Curtis Flood.

Now events have moved so rapidly during these past twenty-four hours that in the interest of clarity I should like to review for you in all its pertinent details, the case of Charles Curtis Flood, who, previous to his disappearance, played baseball right here in Washington, under the alias 'Curt Flood.'

As always, I want to make everything as perfectly clear to you as I can. That is why you hear me say over and over again, in my speeches and press conferences and interviews, that I want to make one thing very clear, or two things, or three things, or as many things as I have on my agenda to make very clear. To give you a little glimpse of the lighter side of the President's life (*impish endearing smile*), my wife tells me that I even say it in my dreams. (*Back to business*) My fellow Americans, I am confident that you recognize as well as I do, that any man who says he wants to make things perfectly clear as often as I do, both awake and in his sleep, obviously does not have anything to hide.

Now who is this man who calls himself 'Curt Flood'? To many Americans, particularly the wonderful mothers of our land, that name is probably as strange as the name Eric Starvo Galt, which, you may remember, was the alias taken by James

Earl Ray, the convicted murderer of Martin Luther King.

Who is 'Curt Flood'? Well, until a year or so ago, the answer would have been simple enough. Flood was a baseball player for the St. Louis Cardinals of the National League, a center fielder with a more than respectable lifetime batting average of .294. Not a Hall of Famer, not the best baseball player in the big leagues, but far from the worst. Many even believed that his finest years lay ahead of him. I am proud to say that I, as an avid fan of baseball as well as all manly sports, was among them.

Then tragedy struck. In 1970, with no more warning than the Japanese gave at Pearl Harbor, 'Curt Flood,' as he then called himself, turned upon the very sport that had made him one of the highest-paid Negroes in the history of our country. In 1970, he announced—and this is an exact quotation from his own writings—'Somebody needs to go up against the system,' and proceeded to bring a legal action against Organized Baseball. According to the Commissioner of Baseball himself, this action would destroy the game of baseball as we know it, if Flood were to emerge victorious.

Now no one expects ordinary citizens, who earn their livelihoods outside the legal profession, to be able to wade through the intricacies of a legal suit such as this fugitive from justice has brought against our great national pastime for the purpose of destroying it. That's why people hire lawyers in the first place. I know when I was a lawyer that was why people hired me, and I think without boasting, that I was able to help them. When I was a young, struggling lawyer, and Pitter and I were living on nine dollars a week out in Prissier, California, which is right here (*points*), I would read through my lawbooks and study long into the night in order to help my clients, most of whom were wonderful young people just like Pitter and myself. At that time, by the way, I had the following debts outstanding:

—$1,000 on our neat little house.
—$200 to my dear parents.
—$110 to my loyal and devoted brother.

—$15 to our fine dentist, a warm-hearted Jewish man for whom we had the greatest respect.

—$4.35 to our kindly grocer, an old Italian who always had a good word for everybody. I still remember his name. Tony.

—75 cents to our Chinese laundryman, a slightly-built fellow who nonetheless worked long into the night over his shirts, just as I did over my law-books, so that his children might one day attend the college of their choice. I am sure they have grown up to be fine and outstanding Chinese-Americans.

—60 cents to the Polish man, or Polack, as the Vice President would affectionately call him, who delivered the ice for our old-fashioned icebox. He was a strong man with great pride in his native Poland.

We also owed moneys amounting to $2.90 to a wonderful Irish plumber, a wonderful Japanese-American handyman and a wonderful couple from the deep South who happened to be of the same race as we were, and whose children played with ours in perfect harmony, despite the fact that they were from another region.

I am proud to say that every last dime that we owed to these wonderful people, I paid back through long hard hours of work in my law office. And the point I wish to make to you tonight, my fellow Americans, is that because of those long, hard hours of work, I believe myself qualified today to understand in all its cunning and clever intricacies the legal action that this fugitive has brought against the sport made famous by Babe Ruth, Lou Gehrig, Ty Cobb, Tris Speaker, Rogers Hornsby, Honus Wagner, Walter Johnson, Christy Mathewson and Ted Williams—Hall of Famers all, and men that America can well be proud of.

And let me tell you this: having studied this case in all its ramifications, I find I can only concur in the wise opinion of the Commissioner of Baseball when he says that a victory for this fugitive would inevitably lead to the death of the great game that has probably done more to make American boys into strong, decent and law-abiding men than any single institution in the land. Frankly, I do not know of a better way for our enemies to undermine the youth of this country, than to destroy this game of baseball and all it represents.

Now there is another question you may want to ask, and it is this: 'Mr. President, if Curt Flood is out to undermine the youth of this country by destroying baseball, where could he possibly find a lawyer who would be willing to take his case to court?'

Now I am going to be as forthright as I know how in answering that question.

Scrupulous and honest and dedicated to the principles of justice as ninety-nine and nine-tenths of the lawyers in this country are, there is in my profession, as in any other, I'm afraid, that tiny percentage who will do and say anything if the stakes are high enough or the price is right. In law school our professors used to call them 'ambulance-chasers' and 'shysters.' Unfortunately, these men cling not only to the bottom rungs of the profession, which would be bad enough, but on rare occasions manage to climb to the very top—yes, even to positions of great responsibility and power.

Now I needn't remind you of the scandal that took place here in Washington during the tenure of the last administration. You all remember that a lawyer appointed by my predecessor to the Supreme Court of the United States, the highest court in the entire land, had to resign as a justice of that court because of financial wrongdoing. Horrifying as that incident was to every decent American, there seems to me nothing to be gained now by reawakening the sense of moral outrage that swept the nation at that time.

As some of you will be quick to point out, there were actually *two* men who found it necessary to resign from the Supreme Court, after they had been appointed justices of that court by my predecessor. But whether there was one, two, three, four or five, I simply do not believe it is in the interests of national unity to harp upon the errors, grievous though they were, of an administration that you voters, in your wisdom, repudiated three years ago.

What is past is past; no one knows that better than I do. If I recall to you now the names of these two men who found it necessary to tender unprecedented resignations to the highest court in the land, it is only to answer, as forthrightly as I know how, your question, 'What kind of lawyer would represent Curt Flood?'

The two men who resigned from the Supreme Court were Mr. Abe Fortas and Mr. Arthur Goldberg. My fellow Americans, the name of the lawyer representing Charles Curtis Flood is Arthur Goldberg. G-o-l-d-b-e-r-g.

Now, before I am accused of trying to shock or alarm the American public, let me say that I myself am not the least bit shocked or alarmed by this turn of events. Having served on the highest court of the land, Mr. Goldberg undoubtedly now knows the ins and the outs of the law as well as the most devious lawyer in the country. Moreover, none of us should be surprised to discover a man who has fallen from the pinnacle of his profession, willing to try just about anything to get back into the public eye. Before the Flood case is concluded, I would not be surprised to find Mr. Abe Fortas joining forces with Mr. Arthur Goldberg in defense of Charles Curtis Flood.

Now you may say to me, 'But surely, Mr. President, any man who wishes to destroy the game of baseball, and enlists such attorneys as these in his attempt to accomplish that end, is not even *entitled* to a hearing in court. Not only is he making a mockery of our entire judicial system, but in order for him to go "up against the system" we, the American taxpayers, have to pay for the upkeep of the very system he is working to annihilate. If we allow that, then we might as well allow self-confessed Communists to teach our children in the classrooms. We might as well throw down our arms right now in the battle for freedom, and hand over our schools and our courtrooms without a fight to the avowed enemies of democracy.'

Well, let me assure you that I couldn't agree more. In fact, we are right now studying ways of restoring the dignity and majesty and sanctity of old to the courtrooms of the land. As you know, one experiment that we have tried with some success here in Washington is the 'Justice in the Streets Program.' This is a program whereby sentencing and punishment, for capital crimes as well as felonies and misdemeanors, is delivered on the spot at the very moment the crime is committed, or even appears to have been committed. Through J.I.T.S.P. and related methods of expediting the judicial process, we hope to be able not only to unclog the court calendars but to wind down the whole trial system by Election Day 1972.

Now, winding down the trial system will of course be a great boon to the dignity of our judges, who will no longer be forced to demean themselves by dealing with the most undesirable elements in the population. Our judges, so terribly overworked as they are today, hopefully will not have to deal with *any* elements of the population once the trial system is completely phased out. This will leave them free for the reflection and reading that is so essential to maintaining a high level of judicial wisdom.

The second benefit to be derived from replacing the archaic and slow-moving trial system by more modern judicial methods is this: the courtrooms of this land will once again be a wonderfully inspiring place for the schoolchildren of America to visit. I see a day, in fact, when parents will be able to send their children off to visit a courtroom without fear that they will have to witness anything inappropriate or unsettling to the eyes or ears of a growing youngster. I see a day in which not only schoolchildren, but mothers holding their babies, will be able to walk through the halls of justice to observe the judges in their wonderful black robes, relieved of the time-consuming burdens of the courtroom, gathering the wisdom of the ages from their thinking and their lawbooks. I see a day when schoolchildren and mothers holding their babies will be able to sit in the jury boxes, just as though a real trial were underway, and in this way experience at firsthand the age-old grandeur of a legal tradition that has come down to us in all its glory from Anglo-Saxon times.

But of course we cannot undo overnight the judicial mess that we have inherited from the previous administration, and the thirty-five administrations before his. As a result, even as we are winding down the trial system that has caused this country so much expense and confusion, we have still to deal in the courtroom with the likes of Charles Curtis Flood and his team of attorneys.

Now fortunately two different courts have already found *against* Charles Curtis Flood in his attempt to destroy the game of baseball. These decisions made during the tenure in office of this administration, have gone a long way, I am sure, to restoring the confidence of a public only recently so disappointed by the verdict reached in Mayor John Lancelot's New York, to free thirteen members of the Black Panther Party.

Of course I have no more right to tell the Mayor of New York how to run his city than he has to tell me how to run the country or the world. But I must, in all honesty, say that I was as startled as the great majority of Americans, first by that verdict, and second, by Mayor Lancelot's decision, following the verdict, to allow these thirteen Black Panthers to resume their political activities in his city. All I can say as President is that I trust this will not become the model for the treatment of the acquitted in other cities around the country.

Now I have no doubt that if the Mayor of New York were in my place he would not hesitate to declare a hands-off policy where Charles Curtis Flood is concerned. If self-confessed Black Panthers are to be left free to stalk the streets that are no longer safe for our wives and daughters, why bother to bring to justice a man who has *not* confessed to being a Black Panther? So, I am afraid, the logic would run, if another man were in my shoes.

But so long as he is not, so long as I am the duly elected President of the United States, I can assure you that there will be no mollycoddling of any fugitive who, after twice being prevented by the courts from destroying baseball and undermining the youth of this country, decided that he, Charles Curtis Flood, had had enough of law and order and life within the system. There will be no mollycoddling of a man who undertook to subvert and corrupt the youth of this country by the most insidious means imaginable, with a recklessness and a

78

viciousness equalled not even by the most hardened drug pushers and the most loathsome pornographers.

No, it was not to the dissolute, unprincipled and over-indulged on our college campuses that Charles Curtis Flood turned with his plan to destroy America. Nor was this yet another call to violence to the dropouts and hippies and flag-defilers of the left.

Who then, you ask, did he seek to corrupt? The answer, my fellow Americans, is the Boy Scouts of America. Not only did Charles Curtis Flood incite them to riot, and tamper with their morals, but what is even worse, it was he and he alone who drove the Boy Scouts headlong into the tragedy that occurred here yesterday in Washington, D.C.

Surely the great majority of Americans will agree that it is a tragedy in every sense of the word when the brave fighting men of our Army are called upon to risk their lives in the streets of Washington, D.C., instead of in a foreign country. But that is what happened here in the nation's capital, when, through a long day and a long night, our brave soldiers, armed only with loaded rifles, fixed bayonets, tear-gas canisters and gas masks, faced a mob of Boy Scouts, numbering nearly ten thousand.

I am sure you all know by now the nature of the chants and the songs that these ten thousand Boy Scouts were singing in the streets of the nation's capital. I am sure you are familiar with the king of placards they were waving before the tele-vision cameras. I do not intend to repeat to you the wording of those posters. It should suffice to say that they did justice to the language and interests of Charles Curtis Flood, whose favorite city, according to his own writings, is Copenhagen, Denmark, the pornography capital of the world.

The posters are presently in the hands of the FBI, whose laboratories have already begun the painstaking job of finger-printing each and every poster, and submitting them to blood tests so as to determine the correlation between the obscenity printed on an individual poster and the blood type of the Boy Scout bearing the poster containing those objectionable words.

If such correlations can be established with a reasonable degree of accuracy—and we think they can—it will of course be of great assistance to our law enforcement agencies. Under our program of 'preventive detention,' we will be able to round up those with suspect blood types *before* such demonstrations as this even get under way, thus preventing them from violating community standards of decency, and the ordinary everyday rules of courtesy, decorum and good taste that are sacred to the great majority of Americans.

As you all know from the headlines, of the approximately ten thousand Boy Scouts who assembled here in Washington during the two-day uprising to threaten the lives of our brave fighting men, it was necessary to kill only three in order to maintain law and order. That breaks down to one and one-half Scouts dead per diem, while nine thousand nine hundred and ninety-eight and a half Scouts continued to live full and active lives the first day, and nine thousand, nine hundred and ninety-seven the second.

Now I would think that by anyone's standards, a mortality rate in a crisis of this kind of .0003 is a wonderful tribute to the very great restraint with which we were able to confront what could have been a terrible tragedy for our soldiers. Certainly it should give solace to all of those who detest bloodshed as much as I do, and put the lie once and for all to the vicious charge that it was the military and not the Scouts who were responsible for the violence. On the other hand, I think the fact that we did have three Scouts dead by the end of the second day is a good indication of the necessary firmness with which we always try to balance off our very great restraint.

Of course, I am sure the great majority of Americans realize that there is always going to be a small, vocal minority of cavilers and critics, who are never going to be satisfied, no matter how perfectly balanced the restraint and the firmness with which we deal with civil disruptions of this kind. Even if there should be only one person dead over a two-day period, or as little as half a person a day; even if over a two-day period there should be only one person who is slightly *maimed*—these critics will begin to talk as though the tragedy wasn't the overwhelming danger to which tens of thousands of our brave soldiers were subjected, but the maiming of one person out of only ten thousand, and what is more than likely, an out-of-towner who, unlike our brave soldiers, had only to remain at home to stay out of harm's way.

Well, to this small vocal minority, let me make one thing very clear.

I too have great sympathy for the families of the three Boy Scouts who were killed here in Washington. I am a father, and I know full well how important children can be to a man's career; and incidentally, in that connection, a wife. As a matter of fact, my wife and I and our wonderful children had condolence messages prepared for far more than the three who died here, and were prepared to dispatch them on a moment's notice. Throughout the crisis I was in continuous touch with the morgue here in Washington, as I am with the morgues around the country, by a special 'hot line,' and had it been necessary to wire not three, but three thousand such messages, I assure you that my family and I would have seen that those words of sympathy had left the White House before the bodies were even cold. I am proud to say that my wife and my daughters were prepared to work far into the night in order that families less fortunate than our own might have some small comfort in their hour of need. Nor do we intend to forget these people when Christmas time rolls around.

But let there be no mistake about it: quick on the trigger as I may be with compassion for the innocent families, I am equally swift in my condemnation of these three guilty Scouts. And I say 'guilty' because if they were not guilty they would not be dead. That is not the kind of country we live in.

Now I know there are those apologists for the Boy Scout uprising who have attempted to arouse sympathy for the three guilty Scouts by pointing out that while one had attained the rank of Eagle Scout, the other two were 'only' Tenderfoots. If pressed they will concede that an Eagle Scout is a highly trained and disciplined youngster, capable of functioning as a guerrilla insurrectionist because of the various survival tactics he has had to master in order to attain his key position in the

81

Scout infrastructure. But what of the two Tenderfoots, they ask. How could two little Tenderfoots pose so serious a threat to our national security as to make it necessary to kill them?

Well, let me answer that question, my fellow Americans, by showing you the weapons that were found concealed, hanging from the belts, of these 'two little Tenderfoot Scouts' when their bodies were searched by the FBI, the Secret Service, the CIA, the Military Police, the Shore Patrol, the Attorney General's office, the Capitol Police Force, the Police Force of the District of Columbia, as well as by law enforcement officers summoned from around the country, to guarantee the probity and thoroughness of this investigation.

Now I am sure that we all still remember with a sad and mournful heart the 6.5-millimeter Italian carbine rifle purchased for $12.78 from a Chicago mail-order house by President Charisma's assassin, Lee Harvey Oswald, whom I mentioned earlier in connection with James Earl Ray and Charles Curtis Flood. In the mail-order catalog that rifle probably did not appear to be any more sophisticated than the weapon I am about to show you now, or any more capable of changing the course of history. And yet none of us will ever forget the impact it had upon President Charisma's career and my own. I know that to many of you this object that I am holding in my right hand looks as innocent and harmless as that $12.78 mail-order rifle undoubtedly did in the mail-order catalog. But let there be no mistake about it, it is just as effective, if not more so.

Firstly: whereas the rifle that destroyed President Charisma's political career measured forty inches over-all, this knife that I hold here in my hand measures, with the blades sheathed, only four and five-eighths inches. This makes it an ideal weapon to use in public places, as opposed to a forty-inch rifle which might arouse suspicion on a school bus, or in a supermarket, or any of the hundred places where you and your loved ones find yourselves in the course of an ordinary day.

Secondly: it is a far more vicious weapon than an ordinary rifle and, needless to say, does not even begin to approach in humaneness a simple thousand-pound bomb, let alone a

82

nuclear explosive. As one who was raised as a Quaker, you know, I have a particularly strong interest in being humane. That is why, since coming to office, I have done everything I can to get Congress to appropriate money for a weapons system that would make us number one in the world in that department. Surely there is no reason why a country with our scientific and technological resources cannot develop weapons with destructive powers so total and immediate as to guarantee to every man, woman and child on this planet what until now has been reserved for those few fortunate people who die in their sleep, and that is the comfort of passing unknowingly from this life into the next. Now that is the type of death people have dreamed about for themselves since time immemorial, and let it not be recorded that Trick E. Dixon lacked the moral and spiritual idealism to address himself to that dream.

But now let me ask you this, my fellow Americans. What could be further from the kind of painless death for men everywhere that this administration is working so hard to bring about, than that which is experienced by the victim of a knife such as I am holding in my hand? Not only is it necessary to deliver as many as five to ten horrifyingly painful stab wounds in order to kill somebody with a weapon this small, but in order to accomplish this the murderer must exhibit a sustained viciousness, a cold-blooded determination to kill, that, I assure you, would shock and appall a combat-tried B-52 bomber pilot no less than it does you and me.

And let me tell you how they manage that sustained viciousness: unlike our pilots in Vietnam, whose satisfaction consists solely in getting the job done as quickly and thoroughly as possible, and who have no interest at all in whatever cries and moans may happen to arise from those who do not die instantly in the blast, the people who use weapons like these are obviously sadists of the sort who *enjoy* watching the blood run out of their victims, and, incidentally in that connection, hearing the cries of a person in physical torment. Why else would they use a weapon that takes up to half an hour to do the sort of job our pilots accomplish in a split second, and without the groaning and the gore?

Now let's look at the knife closely. I am going to open out the blades one by one, and describe to you the purpose and function of each. You should not be misled by its four and five-eighths inch exterior into imagining that it is simply an instrument designed to kill. Like so many of the weapons carried by guerrilla revolutionaries around the world, it has multiple uses, of which murder of the agonizing and sadistic variety is but one.

Let's begin here, with the smallest of the four blades. In the language of those who employ such weapons, it is known as 'the bottle opener.' I'll tell you how it got that name in a moment. You will observe that it is hook-shaped at the end, and measures one inch and one-eighth. It is employed during the interrogation of prisoners primarily to gouge out one or both of the eyes. It is also used on the soles of the feet, which are sliced open, like so, with the point of the hook. Last, but not least, it is sometimes inserted into the mouth of a prisoner who will not talk, in order to slit the flesh at the upper part of the larynx, between the vocal cords. That opening up there is called the glottis, and 'bottle opener' is derived from 'glottal opener,' the pet name originally attached to the blade by its most cold-blooded practitioners.

This second largest blade, measuring one inch and three-quarters, tapers to a point and probably looks to you to be a miniature bayonet. Do not be fooled by appearances. It has nothing to do with bayonets such as those our brave soldiers found it necessary to fix to their rifles in self-defense during the two-day Boy Scout uprising. This little blade is known as 'the leather punch,' and far from being an instrument of self-defense, it is yet another torture device, along the lines of the bottle opener. As its name suggests, it is used to punch holes in human flesh, or 'leather' as the flesh is called by revolutionaries who consider their enemies to be no more than animals. It will come as no surprise to you to learn that it is most frequently driven into the palms of the hands, much the same way that the nails were in the movie *The Greatest Story Ever Told*.

Now this third blade, an eighth of an inch longer than the leather punch, is also wider and less tapered, and has a flat rather than a pointed end. It is known as 'the screwdriver.' Traditionally, it is inserted into the groove between the nails and the flesh and turned in a rotary fashion, like so. However, we know from intelligence reports that the screwdriver may also on occasion be introduced into bodily apertures, of which the nostrils and the ears are the only ones I shall choose to make mention of on nationwide television. Some of my political opponents may think otherwise—and they have every right to disagree with my position—but I, for one, have never believed it necessary to use bad language to make my point, and I have no intention of resorting to those kinds of tactics in the midst of a major address to the nation.

This last blade of the four is probably the one you're most familiar with from your nightmares. Two inches and three-quarters in length, nine-sixteenths of an inch at its widest point, it has a sharp cutting edge that I shall demonstrate for you on this piece of paper.

Incidentally, it is no accident that printed on this piece of paper is the Preamble to the Constitution, the Bill of Rights and the oft-quoted and much beloved Ten Commandments, with their famous 'Thou shalt nots.' As you all remember, these same Ten Commandments provided the wonderful and inspiring background for another motion picture of great spiritual value that I am sure the great majority of American families enjoyed as much as our family did. I don't think I am too far afield when I say that what you see printed on this sheet of paper (*close-up of paper*) is just about everything we believe in and cherish as a people.

I want you to watch as I demonstrate what this blade can do in a matter of seconds to all that you and I hold near and dear.

(*He slices the piece of paper into one-inch strips and then holds them up for the audience to see*)

Of course you can peel apples with a blade like this, you can slice your potatoes for frying and you can cut up your cucumbers, radishes, tomatoes, onions and celery for salad. And I am sure that those who would seek to exonerate these three Scouts will maintain that it was only to prepare a delicious salad such as I described that they secreted these weapons upon their belts and carried them hundreds of miles across state lines to the nation's capital. I am afraid that whether it is knife-carrying Boy Scouts or card-carrying Communists, there will always be a handful of apologists around to come to their defense.

My fellow Americans, I want to leave it to you, and not to the apologists, to decide. I ask you to look at this knife, with all four of its blades unsheathed, blades capable of inflicting physical torment of a kind that goes all the way back to the Crucifixion and beyond. I ask you to look at this four-pronged instrument of torture. I ask you to look at what just *one* of those blades was able to do to the Preamble to the Constitution, the Bill of Rights and the beloved Ten Commandments. And now I ask you if you think there is anything at all to be said in defense of three Boy Scouts carrying such knives into the nation's capital.

And incidentally, in that connection, these were not the only three Boy Scouts in Washington bearing concealed weapons on their belts. These were only the three we happened to kill. In all, a total of eight thousand four hundred and sixty-three knives, each resembling this one in every last detail, were confiscated during the two days the Scouts were here. That means a grand total of thirty-three thousand, eight hundred and fifty-two blades, or enough blades to torture simultaneously every single resident of Chevy Chase, Maryland, including women and children.

Now you ask, how did we prevent this bloodbath from taking place in Chevy Chase? The answer is by setting up an enclosed camping site for the Scouts who were not shot. The answer is by diverting their attention from violence and lawbreaking by giving them a chance to test their scouting abilities overnight in a wilderness environment without food or shelter.

And let me tell you something: it is to the very great credit of the scouting movement in this country, that once we were able to get these boys off the streets and into a rugged camping situation—and we have the police to thank for volunteering their help in getting all the boys out there—they showed themselves worthy in every way of their famous motto, 'Be Prepared.'

Let's take a look at just a few of their accomplishments:

First, in the absence of toilet facilities, they did a tremendous job in disposing of their waste matter and the leaves they used for personal hygiene.

Next, what little water they had in their canteens, they shared in an admirable way, or so it would seem from the fact that not a single one of the nearly ten thousand died of thirst. Nor did they make the mistake of drinking from, or even daring to bathe in, the pond at the campsite, so familiar were they with the danger signs of sewage and stagnation.

Now anyone familiar with Boy Scouts training could have expected that they would be able to use their kerchiefs as tourniquets to stop one another's bleeding, but few of us believed they could ever do the kind of near professional job they did making splints out of vines and branches and shirts torn up into rags.

As for eating, well, I'm proud to say that by morning they had discovered edible roots and berries we didn't even know were there. And as for warmth, as you could expect, they managed during the night to start several fires in the classic Boy Scout manner of rubbing two sticks together.

In all, what might have been a nightmare for the citizens of Chevy Chase, Maryland, was converted into wonderful scouting experience for the boys themselves, and one that I'm sure they'll remember for a long time to come. I know that when the police vans returned this morning to take them away, many of the boys were reluctant to leave the campsite. So anxious were some to spend another night under the stars, and away from the so-called 'comforts' of civilization such as medical attention, lawyers, telephones and food, that it was necessary for the police to chase after them and literally drag them off the premises and into the waiting trucks. With fewer and fewer opportunities available to our youth for 'roughing it,' this administration naturally takes pride in what we were able to do for these youngsters last night. Moreover, we have given them every assurance that if and when they ever come to Washington again, we will make every effort to provide them with the same facilities, or ones even more primitive, if we can find any.

Now I know that many of you out there across the country are asking yourselves why I should be making such a generous offer to the Scouts. Why do I praise them for their behavior at the campsite? Why am I willing to forgive these youngsters and give them another chance to make a decent start in life? It must seem to those of you who saw the Scouts waving their signs here in the streets of the nation's capital—signs offensive and insulting not only to me but, what is far worse, to my innocent family—that I more than anyone have a right to harbor a grievance against these ten thousand Boy Scouts; and particularly against the three who are now dead and will never be able to come to me like responsible children and apologize for trying to smear my reputation. Why, you may ask, am I so compassionate, judicious, charitable, tolerant and wise, when it was my very own political career that stood to be most damaged by these signs?

Well, those are good and intelligent questions. Let me try to answer them as forthrightly as I know how.

My fellow Americans, it is as simple as this (*quickly passes a sponge over his upper lip and slips it back into his breast pocket*): I would rather be a one-term President than carry a grudge against a lot of twelve- and thirteen-year-old American kids. Oh sure, somebody else might try to make political capital out of a vendetta against these youngsters, calling them hoodlums and bums and rotten applies, but I am afraid I am just too big a man for that. As far as I am concerned, these boys have learned their lesson, as they proved at the campsite; and that goes for the three dead Scouts as well. Even if those three dead boys don't come and apologize, as far as I am concerned the past is past and I for one am willing to forgive and forget. For make no mistake about it: while it is true that

I am strongly opposed to permissiveness, I am just as opposed to vindictiveness. I no more believe in punishing a wrongdoer to excess than I would subscribe to the liberal philosophy that allows a criminal to go merrily on his way, after he has committed a crime.

But of even greater importance, I just don't think we ever cure a disease by treating one of its symptoms. Rather, we must get to the cause of the illness. And certainly you know as well as I do, that the cause of America's problems is not the Boy Scouts of America. Nobody is ever going to believe that, and that is why I don't even attempt to make a case for it.

No, the Boy Scouts of America—and I think this will come as a relief to all of you—are no more guilty of anything than you are or I am. They are just another group of American youngsters who have fallen prey to that small dedicated band of malcontents and revolutionaries who are out to destroy our country by destroying our most important natural resource of all, our wonderful youth. And unless we cut these sources of contagion from our society as swiftly and thoroughly as we would excise a cancer from a living body—and I know we are all united in our opposition to cancer, Democrats and Republicans alike—this disease that has spread even to the Boy Scouts will grow in virulence until it has infected every last child in the land, including your own. And so long as I am President, I am not going to stand idly by while the children of this country come down with cancer, leukemia, or, incidentally, in that connection, muscular dystrophy.

No, it is not the Boy Scouts of America, but the man who incited them to this riot by tampering with their morals who must be made to take the punishment that comes to all who would corrupt the youth of our nation. And that man, my fellow Americans, is the very same fugitive for whom the Pro-Pornography government in Copenhagen is providing refuge at this moment.

Now I cannot divulge to you over nationwide television the overwhelming evidence compiled by the Justice Department and the FBI, linking Charles Curtis Flood to the uprising of the Boy Scouts. We all know, however, the tremendous influence that major league baseball players have over the minds and hearts of the young boys of this nation. I am sure that anyone who remembers how he himself idolized the great ball-players of his youth, will not even *need* the evidence in order to imagine just how Charles Curtis Flood might misuse and mislead these boys for his own subversive ends.

I am afraid that is all I can say to you tonight about the evidence proving Flood's guilt. As one who has practiced law, I am particularly sensitive to the Constitutional rights which every defendant is entitled to. And I certainly do not intend to endanger the chances of a conviction by appearing to try this fugitive on nationwide TV. Once he is returned to America, he will be entitled to a fair trial, despite what he has done, and by a jury that has not been prejudiced against him by so august a person as the President of the United States of America.

Right now, as your President, my duty is to do everything within my power to see that this fugitive from justice is returned to our shores. Of course, we have never expected of Flood that he would voluntarily leave his sanctuary in Denmark, given the kinds of pleasures such a man might feel free to pursue in a country with customs that are hardly those of our own. And if Flood is incapable of tearing himself away from his pleasures so as to face the consequences of his vicious actions, neither has the Pro-Pornography government in Copenhagen done anything whatsoever to force him to surrender himself to the proper authorities for extradition. On the contrary, they have rejected out of hand every legitimate request we have made of them. Even now, with the American Army massed on their borders, the American Navy blockading their coast and the American Marines firmly in control of 'Hamlet's Castle,' they continue to provide him with the same protection from the law that they provide to pornographers and filth peddlers from around the globe.

I know that in the face of such profound contempt for American power and prestige, the great majority of Americans would agree that I have no choice but to order our troops onto Danish soil so as to establish the D.A.R. as the freely elected government in Copenhagen. However, I want to tell you this:

because of my Quaker background, I have, only two hours ago, made one last valiant effort to bring about a peaceful resolution of our differences with Denmark. I am going to conclude my address to you tonight by recounting in some detail the nature of that effort. It is a story of bravery and devotion to country that every American will be proud of. It is a story that will convince the entire world how very far this great nation has gone in its attempt to avoid the armed confrontation that the state of Denmark seems committed to forcing upon us.

My fellow Americans, only two hours before coming on television to address you, I gave the order, as Commander-in-Chief of the Armed Forces meeting his responsibilities, for a fleet of helicopters to make a surprise landing on the large Danish island of Zealand at a spot right here (*points*), only twenty nautical miles from the capital of Copenhagen.

Now I realized how dangerous such a gallant humanitarian effort might be. So did the brave Green Berets and Rangers who volunteered to carry it out. Not only would they have to fly in at treetop level to avoid detection by the Danish radar system, but there was no precise way of telling the exact size of the arsenal that Flood had managed to assemble, with the approval, if not the outright assistance, of the Danish government. Would he resort to poison gas? Would he dare to employ tactical nuclear weapons? There was no way in which our aerial photography could penetrate this man's skull, to see just how far he would go in violating the written and unwritten rules of warfare.

But in that reconnaissance by satellite, as well as by manned and drone aircraft, had established beyond a shadow of a doubt that this was where the fugitive was in hiding; and in that I also knew that there was no way to force the Danish government to return Flood to the United States, short of the armed conflict which I am so opposed to as a Quaker, I proceeded to give the order for this raid to take place.

Designed to capture Flood, remove him by helicopter to Elsinore, and hence by military jet to America, the mission was named, by me, Operation Courage, and assigned to Joint Contingency Task Force Derring-Do.

It is with deep pride, my fellow Americans, that I can now tell you that Operation Courage has been carried out to perfection, exactly in accordance with the meticulously rehearsed schedule drawn up beforehand.

First off, the dangerous flight from Elsinore to the landing site was made in twenty-two minutes and fourteen seconds, precisely according to the plan. Next, the hazardous search of the farmhouse, the outbuildings and the tilled acreage was accomplished in thirty-four minutes and eighteen seconds; in other words, with two full seconds to spare. The ticklish evacuation proceedings required precisely the seven minutes called for in the schedule, and the daring return flight to Elsinore, at treetop level, was accomplished in twenty-two minutes flat. That is not only four seconds under the time allotted, but I am proud to say, a new record for that distance for a Danish domestic helicopter flight. Moreover, our forces returned to safety without sustaining a single casualty. As at Elsinore, the enemy was so completely taken by surprise that they did not fire a single shot.

I am proud to tell you that the intelligence on Operation Courage was equally as impressive as the split-second timing with which this perilous mission was accomplished.

First, the seven blond-haired females who were identified on the aerial photos moving in and out of the farmhouse at all hours of the day were present at the time of the landing. They were found, as expected, in beds scattered throughout the house, and taken immediately into custody for interrogation by the Green Berets, as was the couple claiming to be their 'father' and 'mother.' The blond-haired females found in the beds in various stages of undress ranged in age from seven to eighteen.

Second, the dark round objects visible in the aerial photographs and identified positively by intelligence as watermelons, were no longer in the field, or 'patch,' at the time of the landing, nor was there evidence any longer of the watermelon vines themselves. This has led intelligence to conclude that only hours before the raid, the telltale watermelons were removed and replaced with the ordinary rocks and potato plants found at the time of the landing. Obviously, this constituted a desperate last-minute attempt on the part of the fugitive to avoid detection from the air.

As for the large dark object identified as Charles Curtis Flood himself, apparently at the very last minute he too was replaced with a big black Labrador dog. This was verified when the dog was found romping in the very fields where photographs, taken the previous night, revealed the fugitive exercising by moonlight.

It is to the great credit of the commander in charge of Operation Courage—and represents the highest order of dedication and professionalism—that in order to keep faithfully to the plan, the dog was taken into custody in precisely the same amount of time as had been allotted for the capture of Flood. She was then transported in the command helicopter, bound and under heavy guard, to 'Hamlet's Castle' at Elsinore. However, once the helicopters touched safely down, I immediately gave the order from the White House that the interrogation of the dog was to be suspended, and that she was to be released from her bindings and allowed to roam on a leash in a grassy enclosure on the castle grounds.

My fellow Americans, I can assure you that the friendly treatment that dog is receiving now at the hands of American soldiers is in sharp contrast to the heartlessness and cynicism with which the fugitive himself forced this defenseless animal to serve as his 'stand-in' while he took flight from justice yet again.

Now it had been my hope that I could come before you tonight to tell you that Flood was in the custody of American officials, and that it would not be necessary to take further measures against a recalcitrant and contemptuous Danish government in order to secure his release. And make no mistake about it. If we were not dealing with a man so vicious that he would rather risk the life of an innocent female dog than his own, I could have done just that.

However, even though they were unable to apprehend the fugitive at this time, I should still like to take this opportunity to pay a tribute to the skill, courage and devotion with which

Joint Contingency Task Force Derring-Do carried out Operation Courage. The flawless fashion in which they executed this delicate secret mission was inspirational to all Americans. And surely it must be accounted the most successful single operation of its kind staged thus far in the Danish crisis. The embarrassment alone that we have caused Copenhagen by pointing up the holes in their radar system, will inevitably have a profound effect upon the morale of the Danish people and their armed forces.

My fellow Americans, I am going to conclude my address with the words of a very great man. They were written by the immortal bard and renowned humanitarian, William Shakespeare. Yes, they were written with a quill pen on a piece of parchment hundreds and hundreds of years ago, but probably never have they been so true as they are tonight. This is what Shakespeare said: 'Something,' he said, 'is rotten in the state of Denmark.' Little did the immortal bard know then, how prophetic those words would be in the centuries to come.

My fellow Americans (*here Tricky rises from his chair to sit on the edge of his desk*), something *is* rotten in Denmark—let there be no mistake about it. And if it has now fallen to American boys to step in and eradicate the rottenness that Danish boys are unable to step in and eradicate, I know they will not hesitate to do so. (*Makes fist*) Because we will not watch as the once-great homeland of Hamlet slips down the drain of depravity. (*Looks down*) Instead, with all the might that we can summon in our righteous cause, we shall (*quick friendly glance at ceiling*), with God's help, purge Denmark of corruption, now and for all time. (*Looks for a moment into eternity without batting eyelashes*)

Thank you, and good night.

FIVE

THE ASSASSINATION
OF TRICKY

The President of the United States is dead. We repeat this bulletin. Trick E. Dixon is dead. That is all the information we have at this time.

The White House has refused to comment on an earlier bulletin announcing that the President of the United States is dead. The White House Bilge Secretary says, 'There is no truth whatsoever to reports of the President's death,' but adds that he will not 'categorically' deny the story at this time.

Conflicting stories continue to circulate concerning the death of the President. A second White House announcement has now called attention to the President's schedule for the day, pointing out that no mention is made there of dying. Also released was the President's schedule for tomorrow, wherein there also appears to be no plan on the part of the President or his advisers for him to die. 'I think it would be best,' said the White House Bilge Secretary, 'in the light of these schedules, to wait for a statement, one way or another, from the President himself.'

Reports out of Walter Reed Army Hospital now seem to confirm the earlier bulletin that the President of the United States is dead. Though the circumstances surrounding his death remain unclear, it appears that the President was admitted to Walter Reed late yesterday for surgery. The purpose of the secret operation was to remove the sweat glands from his hip. That is all we know at this time.

The Vice President has flatly denied reports of the President's death. Here is a portion of the Vice President's remarks, made as he was on his way to address the National Yodeling Association:

'Now this is just the kind of reckless rot and rotten recklessness that you can expect from the vile vilifiers who are out to vilify vilely.'

'What of the reports, Mr. Vice President, that he had secretly entered Walter Reed last night to have the sweat glands removed from his hip?'

'Hogwash and hokum. *And* hooliganism. *And* heinous. I spoke to him only five minutes ago and found him fit as a fiddle. This lachrymose lie is a lamentable lollapalooza launched by the lunatic left.'

Unconfirmed reports from Walter Reed Hospital now indicate that the President was found dead at seven A.M. this morning. No word yet on the cause of death, or where he was 'found.' Speculation mounts that death came following surgery for the removal of sweat glands lodged in the hip.

We take you now to Republican National Headquarters, where the chairman of the national committee is meeting with reporters:

'I cannot believe that the great majority of Americans are going to keep this great American from a second term in the White House just because he is dead, no.'

'Then you are admitting, sir, that he *is* dead?'

'I didn't say that at all. I said, I just don't think that his death, if it were to come about between now and the election, would affect his popularity with the great majority of Americans. After all, this isn't the first time you people were ready to call him dead, and here he is, President of the United States.'

'But we meant dead politically.'

'I'm not going to get into a fancy discussion of semantics with you fellas. All I'm saying is that whether these rumors are true or false is not going to affect our campaign plans by one iota. I'd even go so far as to say that if it turns out he actually is a corpse, our margin of victory in '72 will be greater by far than what it was in '68.'

'How do you figure that, Mr. Chairman?'

'Well, I for one just cannot imagine the press of this country, irresponsible and vicious as it may be, going after this man dead and buried with the same kind of virulence they used to go after him alive. Furthermore, as regards the voters themselves, it would seem to me that there is a certain sympathy, a certain warmth that a dead Dixon is going to be able to arouse in the people of this country that he never really was able to summon up when he was living and breathing and so on.'

'If he is dead then, you think it would be good for his image?'

'No doubt about it. I think that in terms of exposure he may have gone about as far as he can alive. This is probably just the shot in the arm we've been looking for, particularly if the Democrats run Teddy Charisma.'

'Can you explain what you mean, Mr. Chairman?'

'Well, assuming for the sake of argument that Trick E. Dixon is no more, that is going to cut strongly into the source of Charisma's appeal. It's one thing, you see, for a candidate for the Presidency to have two brothers who are dead—it's something else when the incumbent *himself* is dead. I mean, if experience is any kind of criterion—and I think it is—I just don't see how you can top the President now, where this whole death issue is concerned.'

'Mr. Chairman, is there any truth at all to the growing suspicion that you people are sending up a trial balloon with these rumors of the President's death? To see just how much political mileage there is in it, if any? That is, on the one hand you yourself sound convinced that the President's death would give a great boost to his waning popularity, while Vice President What's-his-name asserts that the President is "fit as a fiddle" and that these rumors have been propagated by "the lunatic left." '

'Look, I have no intention of criticizing the alliteration of the Vice President of the United States of America. Under the Constitution he has a right to alliterate just as much as any other American citizen. I am speaking to you boys strictly as party chairman, and all I am saying, in language plain and simple, is that the President has absolutely no intention of withdrawing from the race for any reason whatsoever, including his own death. Anybody who counts him out because of something like that, just doesn't know the kind of guy they are dealing with. This isn't a Lyin' B. Johnson, who tosses in the towel because the country hates his guts and doesn't trust him as far as they can throw him. No, you're not going to intimidate Trick E. Dixon just by hating him. Hell, he's had that all his life; he's *used* to it. And you're not going to keep him off the ballot by killing him either. We've seen him rise from the ashes before, and I have every expectation that we are going to see precisely that again. If he has to address that convention from inside an urn, he'll do it—that's the kind of dedicated American we're talking about.'

The White House has now issued a statement denying—I repeat, *denying*—that the President entered Walter Reed Hospital yesterday for the removal of the sweat glands from his hip. There continues however to be a total news blackout from that source as to whether President Dixon is dead or alive.

We take you now to the National Weightlifters Convention, where Vice President What's-his-name is in the midst of an impromptu address on those who he claims have perpetrated upon the nation this 'lachrymose lie':
'the nitwits, the namby-pambys, the neurasthenics, the neurotics, the necrophiliacs——'

We interrupt the Vice President's alliteration to take you to Walter Reed Hospital for a special report:
'The mood here is somber, though it remains impossible to piece the story together in its entirety. It seems now that the President did enter the hospital late yesterday for a secret operation. First reports had it that the operation was to have

been on his hip, for the surgical removal of sweat glands apparently lodged in that area. However, the White House, as you know, has flatly denied that story, and only a moment ago I learned the reason why. The operation was to have been not on the Chief Executive's hip, but on his lip, l-i-p. The sweat glands were, from all reports, to have been removed from the lip this morning. But now, according to the latest White House communiqué, surgery has been postponed for the time being because of, and I quote, 'an unforeseen development.' According to highly placed sources within the hospital itself, that unforseen development is the death of the President of the United States. Now I see that the Secretary of Defense has just emerged from the hospital and is walking this way. Secretary Lard, have you just come from the President's side?'

'Yes.'

'You seem quite despondent, sir. Can you tell us if he is dead or alive?'

'I'm not at liberty to answer that question.'

'Unconfirmed reports from various sources say he was found dead at seven A.M. this morning.'

'No comment.'

'Can you tell us then why you were visiting him?'

'To find out his secret timetable for ending the war.'

'Is there anybody other than the President who knows the secret timetable?'

'Of course not.'

'Then if he's dead, he's taken the secret timetable with him to the grave?'

'No comment.'

'Secretary Lard, did the President have any other visitors aside from yourself?'

'Yes. The Joint Chiefs. And of course the Professor.'

'And they don't know the secret timetable either?'

'I told you, nobody knows it but him. That's what makes it secret.'

'Not even his wife?'

'Well, actually, she thought she had it, when we called her

this morning. But it was just an old train schedule between Washington and New York. She found it in one of his suits.'

'There's no other place he might have left it?'

'It doesn't seem like it.'

'Cut open the mattresses, did you?'

'Oh, all of that. Ripped up floors. Tore out paneling. Turned the place inside out. No sign of anything *resembling* a secret timetable.'

'Mr. Secretary, everything you say seems to confirm the rumor that the President is dead. If that is the case, what were you and the Joint Chiefs and the Professors doing sitting around a corpse, trying to find out vital information?'

'Well, we also had a medium with us.'

'A *medium*?'

'Oh, don't worry. She's worked for us before. Highest security clearance. Top-flight Gypsy.'

'And did she get through to the President?'

'I believe I can say she did.'

'How do you know?'

'Well, she got through to a voice who kept saying he was a Quaker.'

'And what about the secret timetable?'

'He says a secret is a secret, and he owes it to the American people, who have placed their confidence in him, not to betray a sacred trust. He said they can brand and skewer him in Hell, he's never going to tell a soul.'

'Honest almost to a fault.'

'Well, he had to be, you know, with that sweating problem. Otherwise people tended not always to believe everything he said.'

'Ladies and gentlemen, that was the Secretary of Defense, speaking directly from the lawn outside of Walter Reed Hospital. As you saw, he was distraught and very near to tears throughout the interview, thus appearing to confirm the reports of the President's death. We return you to the Vice President, who is now addressing the National Sword Swallowers Association.'

'—the psychotics, the sob sisters, the skin merchants, the saboteurs, the self-styled Sapphos, the self-styled Swinburnes, the swine, the satyrs, the schizos, the sodomists, the sissies, the screamers, the screwy, the scum, the self-congratulatory self-congratulators, the sensationalists, the snakes in the grass, the sex fiends, the shiftless, the shines, the shaggy, the sickly, the syphilitic——'

We go now to the headquarters of the Federal Bureau of Investigation:

'Is it the same knife that the President demonstrated on television last night, Chief?'

'No doubt about it. Here are the four blades. Count 'em. One, two, three, four. Open-and-shut case.'

'But my understanding was that some eight thousand such knives——'

'We've sifted through the eight thousand, don't worry about that. And this is the one. This is the murder weapon, no doubt about it.'

'Then the President has been murdered?'

'I can't tell you that right now. But I can assure you that if there has been a murder, this is what did it.'

'And do you have the murderer in custody?'

'One thing at a time. You rush in and say you've got the murderer, everybody thinks you picked up the first guy you could find out on the street. Let's at least get the announcement of a murder, before we start accusing people.'

'How about the kind of murder. Stabbed to death?'

'Well, there again it's like, "Have you stopped beating your wife." But of course I will say this much: with a knife, you may very well find that the victim has been stabbed to death, yes. Of course, there are other possibilities as well, and I can assure you we're looking into them thoroughly.'

'For instance.'

'Well, you've got your bludgeoning, of course. You've got your various forms of torture such as the President himself outlined on TV the other night.'

'In other words, it's possible the President's famous eyes

101

may have been gouged out.'

'I wouldn't rule that out at this time, no.'

'But by whom? How? When? Where?'

'Look, as we say here at the Bureau, ask me no questions and I'll tell you no lies. The important thing right now is that we want to assure the American people, not only that we are actually on top of this case even before it has broken, but that we are keeping them abreast of the facts virtually before there are any. We just don't intend to come in for the sort of criticism on this assassination of a Presidnt that we did on the last one.'

'What sort of criticism do you mean?'

'Well, last time there was just some kind of cloud over the whole thing, wasn't there? Credibility gap and so on. People thinking they weren't getting the straight story. Accusing us of covering up and being caught off guard and so on. Well, this time it's going to be different, I can assure you. This time we have the weapon and a fairly good idea of who did it beforehand, and we're really only waiting for word that it actually happened, to make an arrest. After a decent interval, of course, just so it doesn't look as though we picked up the first poor slob we found in the gutter.'

'Is it a Boy Scout? That is, will it be a Boy Scout, if and when?'

'Well, of course I am only a law enforcement officer. I don't decide who commits the crimes, I just catch them, after that decision has been made by the proper authorities. I will say this, however. We would not have decided on a Boy Scout knife as the murder weapon, if we didn't think there was a good strong motive to go with it. That was one of the troubles with the last assassination: didn't have a good strong motive to go with it. After all, we are talking about the assassination of the highest elected officer in the land. People like a good strong motive when something like that happens, and I can't say that I blame them. That's why this time we intend to give it to them. Otherwise, you're just going to get your national disunity, your credibility gap, your doubt, and your cloud over the whole thing.'

'And you honestly think that this Boy Scout knife will clear up such doubt and incredulity?'

'Why? Don't you?'

'Well, it's not for me to say. I'm just an objective reporter.'

'No, no, go ahead, *say*. What do you think? Just because you're objective doesn't necessarily make you a fool. You don't find the Boy Scout knife convincing? Is that it?'

'But what I think isn't at issue—either this is or is not the murder weapon.'

'In other words, you're implying that it does seem to you far-fetched. Good enough. What would you think of this, then?'

'*That?*'

'Yes, sir—a Louisville Slugger. Curt Flood's very own baseball bat. Let me show you on this model here of the President's head the kind of damage you can do with one of these things. Remember, before, when I said "bludgeoned"? Well, watch this.'

To the White House now, for an important announcement by the President's Bilge Secretary.

'Ladies and gentlemen, I'd like to make the following announcement concerning the President's health. At midnight last night the President entered Walter Reed Army Hospital for minor surgery involving the surgical removal of the sweat glands from his upper lip.'

'Can you spell that, Blurb?'

'Lip. L-i-p.'

'And the first word?'

'Upper. U-p-p-e-r ... Now as you know, the President has always wanted to do everything he could to gain the trust and the confidence and, if it was within the realm of possibility, the affection of the American people. It was his belief that if he could stop sweating so much along his upper lip when he addressed the nation, the great majority of the American people would come to believe he was an honest man, speaking the truth, and maybe even like him a little better. Now this is not to say that people who sweat along the upper lip are necessarily liars and/or unlikable. Many people who sweat profusely along the upper lip are outstanding citizens in their communities and sweat the way they do because of the many civic duties they are called upon to perform. Then too there are a lot of good, hard-working ordinary citizens who simply sweat along the upper lip as a matter of course ... That is really all I have to say to you at this hour, ladies and gentlemen. I wouldn't have bothered to call you together like this, had it not been for the continuing rumors that it was the President's "hip" that had required surgery. There is absolutely no truth to that whatsoever, and I wanted you to be the first to know. I hope by tomorrow in fact to have available for you x-ray photos of the President's hip that will make it absolutely clear that it is in perfect condition.'

'Which hip will that be, Blurb?'

'The left hip.'

'What about the right one?'

'We'll try to get those to you within the week. I assure you that we're working to clear this thing up just as fast as we can. We don't want the people in this country to go around thinking the President has something wrong with his hips any more than you do.'

'What about the reports that he's dead, Blurb?'

'I have nothing to say about that at this time.'

'But Secretary Lard was seen weeping as he left Walter Reed today. Surely that suggests that President Dixon is dead.'

'Not necessarily. It could just as well mean that he's alive. I'm not going to speculate either way, gentlemen, in a matter this serious.'

'What about reports that he's been murdered by a Boy Scout gone berserk?'

'We're looking into that, and if there's any truth at all to that story, I assure you, we'll be in touch with you about it.'

'Can you say anything definite about his condition at all?'

'He's resting comfortably.'

'Are the sweat glands out? And if so, can we see them?'

'No comment. Moreover, it would really be up to the First Lady anyway, whether she wanted the President's sweat glands to be made available for photographs and so on. I think she might want to keep something as personal as those glands just for the immediate family, and maybe eventually build a Trick E. Dixon Library at Prissier in which to house them.'

'Can you tell us how big they are, Blurb?'

'Well, I would imagine that given the sheer amount of sweating he used to do, they were pretty good-sized. But I'm only guessing. I haven't seen them.'

'Blurb, is there any truth to the report that while at Walter Reed he was also going to have surgery done to prevent his eyes from shifting?'

'No comment.'

'Does that mean they *were* gouged out?'

'No comment.'

'Will the eyes be in the Trick E. Dixon Library at Prissier too, Blurb?'

'Once again, that would be entirely up to the First Lady.'

'Blurb, what about his gestures? He's been criticized for a certain unnaturalness, or falseness, in his gestures. They don't always seem tied in to what he's saying. If he's still alive, are there any plans for him to have that fixed too? And if so, how? Can they sort of get him synchronized in that department?'

'Gentlemen, I'm sure the doctors are going to do everything they can to make him appear as honest as possible.'

'One last question, Blurb. If he's dead, that would make Mr. What's-his-name the President. Is there any truth to the rumor that you people are postponing the announcement of Dixon's death because you're looking for a last-minute replacement for What's-his-name? Is that why Mr. What's-his-name himself keeps denying so vehemently the reports that the President is dead—for fear of being dumped?'

'Gentlemen, I think you know as well as I do that the Vice President is not the kind of man who would want to be President of the United States if he felt there was any doubt as to his qualifications for the office. That's not even a question I will take seriously.'

'Good evening. This is Erect Severehead with a cogent news

analysis from the nation's capital ... A hushed hush pervades the corridors of power. Great men whisper whispers while a stunned capital awaits. Even the cherry blossoms along the Potomac seem to sense the magnitude. And magnitude there is. Yet magnitude there has been before, and the nation has survived. A mood of cautious optimism surged forward just at dusk. Then set the age-old sun behind these edifices of reason, and gloom once more descended. Yet gloom there has been, and in the end the nation has survived. For the principles are everlasting, though the men be mortal. And it is that very mortality that the men in the corridors of power. For no one dares to play politics with the momentousness of a tragedy of such scope, or the scope of a tragedy of such momentousness. If tragedy it be. Yet tragedies there have been, and the nation founded upon hope and trust in man and the deity, has continued to survive. Still, in this worried capital tonight, men watch and men wait. So too do women and children in this worried capital tonight watch and wait. This is Erect Severehead from Washington, D.C.'

'——the flag-burners, the faggots, the fairies, the filth peddlers, the Fabian Socialists of yore, the fair-weather friends, the fairies, the faithless, the flesh-show operators——'

We interrupt the Vice President's address to the National Primates Association to bring you the following bulletin. A troop of Boy Scouts from Boston, Massachusetts, the home state of Senator Edward Charisma, has confessed to the murder of the President of the United States. The FBI has declined to give their names until such time as the President's murder has been announced by the White House. The Boy Scouts are being held without bail, and according to the FBI the case is, quote cinched unquote. The murder weapon, which at first was believed to be the very knife that the President had exhibited on television during his famous 'Something Is Rotten in Denmark' speech, is now identified as a Louisville Slugger baseball bat, formerly the property of Washington Senator center fielder Curt Flood. We return you to Vice

President What's-his-name at the Primates convention:

'—the flotsam and jetsam of the universities, the fairies, the folk singers, the fairies, the freaks, the fairies, the free-loaders on welfare, the fairies, the free-speechers with their favorite four-letter word, the fairies——'

We switch you to our correspondent at Walter Reed Army Hospital.

'Ladies and gentlemen, this terrible news has just come to us from a highly reliable source within the hospital. The President of the United States was assassinated sometime in the early hours of the morning. The cause of death was drowning. He was found at seven A.M., unclothed and bent into the fetal position, inside a large transparent baggie filled with a clear fluid presumed to be water, and tied shut at the top. The baggie containing the body of the President was found on the floor of the hospital delivery room. How he was removed from his own room, where he was awaiting surgery on his upper lip, and forced or enticed into a baggie is not known at this time. There would seem to be little doubt, however, that the manner in which he has been murdered is directly related to the controversial remarks he made at San Dementia on April 3, in which he came out four-square for "the rights of the unborn."

'Right now, hospital officials seem to believe that the President left his bed voluntarily to accompany his assailant to the delivery room, perhaps in the belief that he was to be photographed there beside the stomach of a woman in labor. The recent Scout uprising, and yesterday's nuclear bombing of Copenhagen, seemed to those of us here in Washington to have taken something of an edge off his campaign in behalf of the unborn, and it may well be that he had decided to seize upon this fortuitous circumstance to revitalize interest in his program. Doubtless, with the destruction of Copenhagen and the occupation of Denmark successfully accomplished, he was anxious to return to what he considered our most pressing domestic problem. Rumor has it that he intended, in his next major address, to use his new upper lip to outline his belief in "the sanctity of human life, including the life of the yet unborn."

'But now there will be no speech on the sanctity of human life with the new lip he would have been so proud of. A cruel assassin with a macabre sense of humor has seen to that. The man who believed in the unborn is dead, his unclothed body found stuffed in the fetal position inside a water-filled baggie on the floor of the delivery room here at Walter Reed Hospital. This is Roger Rising-to-the-Occasion at Walter Reed.'

Quickly now to the White House, and the latest bulletin from the Bilge Secretary.

'Ladies and gentlemen, I have a few more facts for you now about the President's hip, including the x-ray I promised earlier. This gentleman in white that you see beside me in his surgical gloves, gown and mask is probably the foremost authority on the left hip in the world. Doctor, will you comment on this x-ray of the President's left hip for the members of the press. I'll hold it for you so you don't dirty your gloves.'

'Thank you, Blurb. Ladies and gentlemen, there is just no doubt about it in my mind. This is a left hip.'

'Thank you, Doctor. Any questions?'

'Blurb, the report from Walter Reed is that the President has been assassinated. Stuffed naked into a baggie and drowned.

'Gentlemen, let's try to keep to the subject. The doctor here has flown in from Minnesota right in the middle of an operation on a lift hip, to verify this x-ray for you. I don't think we want to keep him longer than we have to. Yes?'

'Doctor, can you be absolutely sure that the left hip is the President's?'

'Of course I can.'

'How, sir?'

'Because that's what the Bilge Secretary said it was. Why would he give me a picture of a hip and say it was the President's if it wasn't?'

'—the gadflies, the go-go girls, the geldings, the gibbons, the gonadless, the gonorrhea-carriers——'

We interrupt the Vice President's address to the National Association for the Advancement of Color Slides to switch you to our correspondents around the country.

First, Morton Momentous in Chicago:

'Here in the Windy City the mood is one of incredulity, of shock, of utter disbelief. So stunned are the people of this great Middle Western metropolis that they seem totally unable to respond to the bulletins from Washington that have come to them over radio and television. And so from the Gold Coast to Skid Row, from the fashionable suburbs of the North to the squalid ghettos of the South, the scene is much the same: people going about their ordinary, everyday affairs as though nothing had happened. Not even the flags have been lowered to half-staff, but continue to flutter high in the breeze, even as they did before the news reached this grief-stricken city of the terrible fate that has befallen our leader. Trick E. Dixon is dead, cruelly and bizarrely murdered, a martyr to the unborn the world round—and it is more than the mind or spirit of Chicago can accept or understand. And so throughout this great city, life, in a manner of speaking, goes on—much as you see it directly behind me here in the world-famous Loop. Shoppers rushing to and fro. The din of traffic continuous. Restaurants jammed. Streetcars and busses packed. Yes, the frantic, mindless scurrying of a big city at the rush hour. It is almost as though the people here in Chicago are afraid to turn for a single second from the ordinary routine of an ordinary day, to face this ghastly tragedy. This is Morton Momentous from a stunned, incredulous Chicago.'

We take you now to Los Angeles and correspondent Peter Pious.

'If the people in the streets of Chicago are incredulous, you can well imagine the mood of the ordinary man in the pool here in Trick E. Dixon's native state. In Chicago they are simply unable to respond; here it is even more heart-rending. The Californians I have spoken with—or tried to speak with—are like nothing so much as small children who have been confronted with an event far beyond their emotional range of response. All they can do when they learn the tragic news that Trick E. Dixon has been found stuffed in a baggie is giggle. To be sure, there are the proverbial California wisecracks, but by and large it is giggling such as one might hear from perplexed and bewildered children that remains in one's ears, long after the giggler himself has dived off the high board or driven away in his sports car. For this is Trick E. Dixon's state and these are Trick E. Dixon's people. Here he is not just the President, here he is a friend and a neighbor, one of them, a healthy child of the sunlight, of the beaches and the blue Pacific, a man who embodied all the robustness and grandeur of America's golden state. And now that golden child of the Golden West is gone; and Californians can only giggle to suppress their sobs and hide their tears. Peter Pious in Los Angeles.'

Next, Ike Ironic, in New York City.

'No one ever believed that Trick E. Dixon was beloved in New York City. Yes, he lived here once, in this fashionable Fifth Avenue apartment building directly behind me. But few ever considered him a resident of this city so much as a refugee from Washington, biding his time to return to public office. Nor did New Yorkers seem much impressed when he assumed the powers of the Presidency in 1969. But now he is gone, and all at once the very deep affection, the love, if you will, for their former neighbor, is everywhere apparent. Of course, you have to know New Yorkers to be able to penetrate the outer shell of cynicism and see the love beneath. You had to look, but you saw it today, here in New York: in the seeming boredom and indifference of a bus driver; in the impatience of a salesgirl; in the anger over nothing of a taxi driver; in the weariness of the homebound workers packed into the subway; in the blank gaze of the drunks along the Bowery; in the haughtiness of a dowager refusing to curb her dog on the fashionable Upper East Side. You had to look, but there it was, love for Trick E. Dixon ... Only now he is gone, gone

110

before they could, with their boredom and indifference and impatience and anger and exhaustion and blankness and haughtiness, express to him all they felt so deeply in their hearts. Yes, the bitter irony is this: he had to die in a baggie, before New Yorkers could tender him that hard-won love that would have meant so much to him. But then it is a day of bitter ironies. Ike Ironic from grief-stricken and, perhaps, guilt-ridden Fifth Avenue in the city of New York, where he lived like a stranger, but has died like a long-lost son.'

Reports coming in from around the nation confirm those you have just heard from our correspondents in Chicago, Los Angeles and New York, reports of people too stunned or heartbroken to be able to respond with the conventional tears or words of sorrow to the news of President's Dixon's assassination. No, the ordinary signs of grief are clearly not sufficient to express the emotion that they feel at this hour, and so they pretend for the time being that it simply has not happened; or they giggle with embarrassment and disbelief; or they attempt to hide beneath a gruff exterior, the deep love for a fallen leader that smolders away within.

And what of the madman who perpetrated this deed? For that story, we return you to the headquarters of the FBI in Washington.

'That's right, we're pretty sure now it was a madman who perpetrated this deed.'

'And the Scouts? The knife? The Louisville Slugger?'

'Oh, we're not ruling out any of the hard evidence. I'm talking now about the brains behind the whole thing. More accurately, the lack of brains. You see, that's really our number one clue—everything else aside, this was a pretty stupid thing to do to the President. There he is, the President, and they do a stupid thing like this. Now if this is somebody's idea of a practical joke, well, I for one don't consider it funny. You're not just stuffing *anybody* into a baggie, you're stuffing the President of the United States. What about the dignity of his office? If you have no respect for the man, what about the office? That's what really gravels me, personally. I mean, what do you think the enemies of democracy would think if they saw the President of the United States all curled up naked like that. Well, I'll tell you what they'd think: they couldn't be happier. That's just the kind of propaganda they love to use to brainwash people and make Communists out of them.'

'Do you think then that the assassin was an enemy of democracy as well as a madman?'

'I do. And as I said, a practical joker. Fortunately, we happen to have a complete file on all madmen who are enemies of democracy and practical jokers, and they're under constant surveillance. So I don't think there's going to be any trouble finding our man, or madman. And even if we don't find him, we've got the Boy Scouts from Boston who confessed to this thing in reserve, so I'd say, on the whole, we're in much better shape than we were last time, and are really just waiting a go-ahead from the White House...'

'We are privileged to have with us in the studio one of the most distinguished members of the House of Representatives, a leading Republican statesman, and a friend and confidant to the late President. Congressman Fraud, this is a sorrowful day in our nation's history.'

'Oh, it's a day that will live in infamy, there's no doubt about that in my mind. I am, in fact, introducing a bill into Congress to have it declared a day that will live in infamy and celebrated as such in coming years. What you've got here, as Chief Heehaw at the FBI was saying, is a real lack of respect for the office of the Presidency. What you've got here in this assassin is a very disrespectful person, and, I would agree, probably a madman to boot.'

'Do you have any idea, Congressman, why the White House continues at this late hour to refuse to confirm the story of the assassination?'

'I think it goes without saying that we're in a sensitive area here, and consequently they want to move cautiously on this whole thing. I think they want, first off, to gauge the public reaction here at home, and then of course there is the reaction around the world to consider. On the one hand you've got our allies who depend upon us for support, and on the other hand you've got our enemies who are always on the lookout for some chink in our armor, and if you keep all that in mind, then I think you have to agree that in the long run it is probably in the interest of our integrity and our credibility to cover this whole thing up. I would think that some such reasoning as that is going on behind the scenes at the White House right now.'

'Has the First Lady been notified?'

'Oh, of course.'

'What was her reaction?'

'Well, she was understandably quite overcome in the first moment. But, as you know, she is a very decorous woman, even in moments of great emotion. Consequently, her immediate reaction was to note that the manner in which the assassin went about the assassination was in extremely bad taste. The baggie aside for the moment, she thinks that at the very least the President should have been slain in a shirt and a tie and a jacket, like John F. Charisma. She says there was a suit fresh from the dry cleaners in the closet at the hospital, and that it really shows that the assassin was a person of very poor breeding to have failed to recognize how important it is for the President, of all people, to be neatly and appropriately garbed at all times. She said she just had to wonder about the upbringing of a person who would forget something like that. She said she didn't want to blame the assassin's family, until she knew all the facts, but it was clear she felt there probably could have been a wee bit more attention given to good grooming in his house when the assassin was growing up.'

'Congressman Fraud, there has been some speculation that the President's assassination is a reprisal for the destruction yesterday of the city of Copenhagen. What do you think of that idea?'

'Not very much.'

'Can you explain?'

'Well, it just doesn't make any sense. The President himself went on television, after all, and explained to the American people the situation in Denmark and why we might have to destroy Copenhagen. Now he didn't have to do that, you know—but he did, because he wanted the people to have all the facts. So I just don't see how you can fault him there. And, I must say, in praise of this great country, that except for a few elderly people out there in Wisconsin—and they of course turned out to be of Danish extraction, and obviously didn't have any objectivity on this matter at all—but except for those few irresponsible demonstrators out there shouting dirty words in Danish, the overwhelming majority of the people of this country have taken the destruction of Copenhagen with the wonderful equanimity and solidarity we have come to expect of them in matters like this. No, I just can't see where somebody is going to assassinate the President for a sound policy decision such as this one, and that even goes for a madman. No, he had the mandate of the people here, lunatics included.'

'And the mandate of the Congress as well?'

'Well, of course, as you know, there are unfortunately a very few Congressmen and Senators—I guess you could call them headline seekers—who will go so far as to try to make political hay out of the bombing of a little God-forsaken village out in the middle of nowhere, some crossroads nobody has ever heard of before and surely after the bombing will never hear of again—so I leave it to you to imagine what such politicians are going to do with the nuclear destruction of a place like Copenhagen. In their behalf, however, let me say that even *they* would not be so reckless as to assassinate the President because of a difference of opinion over something like bombing sites. I mean, nobody's perfect. One President chooses this target, one President chooses that target, but fortunately we have in this country a political system that can accommodate itself to that kind of disagreement, without recourse to assassination. And by and large I think you can say that in the end the mistakes in judgment and so on shake themselves out, and we pretty much destroy the places that need destroying. It seems to me, in fact, that as regards the destruction of Copenhagen, you'll find that even among the President's staunchest critics in the Senate, there was a sense that a decision of that magnitude simply couldn't have been arrived at lightly or arbitrarily. I think most of the truly responsible members of the Congress

114

feel as I do, that having made a strong show of strength such as this in Scandinavia now, we are not going to get ourselves bogged down there later the way we did in Southeast Asia.'

'So you see no connection between the "Something Is Rotten in Denmark" speech and the assassination?'

'No, no. Frankly I can't believe that the murder of the President has to do with anything he has ever said *or* done, including his courageous remarks in behalf of the unborn and the sanctity of human life. No, this is one of those wild, crazy acts, just as the FBI describes it—the work of a madman, and, as the First Lady suggests, a pretty ill-mannered madman, at that. It seems to me that any attempt to find some rational political motive in anything so bizarre and boorish as stuffing the President of the United States unclothed into a water-filled baggie in the fetal position is so much wasted effort. It's an act of violence and disrespect, utterly without rhyme or reason, and cannot but arouse the righteous indignation of reasonable and sensible men everywhere.'

'—the hairy, the half-cocked if you know what I mean, the hammer-and-sickle supporters, the hard-core pornographers, the hedonists, the Hell's Angels, those whom God won't help because they won't help themselves, the hermaphrodites, the highbrows, the hijackers, the hippies, the Hisses, the homos, the hoodlums of all races, the heroin pushers, the hypo-crites——'

'Yes, the tribute has begun, the tribute to the man they loved more than they knew. By trains they come, by busses, by cars, by planes, by wheelchairs, by feet. Come some on canes and crutches, and some on artificial limbs. But come un-daunted they do, like pilgrims of yesteryear and yore, to honor pay to him they loved more than they knew. Reaped by the Grim Reaper before his reaping was due, he brings us together at last, as he promised he one day would do. And doing it he is. For in they come, the ordinary people, *his* people, barbers and butchers and brokers and barkers, tycoons and taxider-mists and the taciturn who till the land. It is, I daresay, a

115

demonstration the likes of which he who has been grimly reaped by the Grim Reaper did not, alas, survive to witness. No, during his brief residence on this planet Earth, and his three years in the White House, they demonstrated not to honor him but to humiliate him, not to pay him homage and respect but to shout their obscenities at, and display their disrespect toward, him. But these are not the obscenity-shouters and the disrespect-displayers gathering here tonight along the banks of the Potomac—banks as old as the Republic itself—and beneath the cherry blossoms he so loved, and in the brooding grandeur of this the city which embodies that which he who has been untimely reaped would have himself willingly laid down his life for, had of him it been asked instead of cruelly being stolen in the night from him by an ill-mannered madman with a baggie. Yet madmen there have been and madmen there will be, and still this nation has endured. And, I daresay, endure it will, while the madmen pass through these corridors of power and halls of justice and closets of virtue and dumbwaiters of dignity and cellars of idealism, leaving us in the end, if not stronger, wiser; and if not wiser, stronger; and if, alas, not either, both. This is Erect Severehead with a cogent news analysis from the nation's capital.'

'This is Brad Bathos. I'm down here in the streets of Washington now, and it is a moving and heart-rending sight I see. Ever since the news first broke that the President had been found dead in a baggie at Walter Reed Hospital, the people of this great country, *his* people, have been pouring into the capital from all over the nation. Thousands upon thousands simply standing here in the streets surrounding the White House, with heads bowed, visibly shaken and moved. Many are crying openly, not a few of them grown men. Here is a man seated on the curbstone holding his head in his hands and quietly sobbing. I'm going to ask him if he will tell us where he comes from.'

'I come from here, I come from Washington.'

'You're sitting on the curbstone quietly sobbing into your hands. Can you tell us why? Can you put it into words?'

116

'Guilt.'

'You mean you feel a personal sense of guilt?'

'Yes.'

'Why?'

'Because I did it.'

'*You* did it? *You* killed the President?'

'Yes.'

'Well, look, this is important—have you told the police?'

'I've told everyone. The police. The FBI. I even tried to call Pitter Dixon to tell her. But all they kept saying was that it was kind of me to think of them at a time like this and Mrs. Dixon appreciated my sympathy and thought it was in very good taste, and then they hung up. Meanwhile, I should be *arrested*. I should be in the papers—my picture, and a big headline, DIXON'S MURDERER. But nobody will believe me. Here, here's the notebooks where I've been planning it for months. Here are tape recordings of my own telephone conversations with friends. Here, look at this: a signed confession! And I wasn't even under duress when I wrote it. I was in a hammock. I was fully aware of my constitutional rights. My lawyer was with me, as a matter of fact. We were having a drink. Here—just read it, I give all my reasons and everything.'

'Sir, interesting as your story is, we have to move on. We must move on through this immense crowd . . . Here's a young attractive woman holding a sleeping infant in her arms. She is just standing on the sidewalk gazing blankly at the White House. Heaven only knows how much anguish is concealed in that gaze. Madam, will you tell the television audience what you're thinking about as you look at the White House?'

'He's dead.'

'You appear to be in a state of shock.'

'I know. I didn't think I could do it.'

'Do what?'

'Kill. Murder. He said, "Let me make one thing perfectly——" and before he could say "clear," I had him in the baggie. You should have seen the look on his face when I turned the little twister seal.'

'The look on the President's face when *you*——?'

'Yes. I've never seen such rage in my life. I've never seen such anger and fury. But then he realized I was staring at him through the baggie, and suddenly he looked just the way he does on television, all seriousness and responsibility, and he opened his mouth, I guess to say "clear," and that was it. I think he thought the whole thing was being televised.'

'And—well, was your baby with you, when you allegedly——?'

'Oh yes, yes. Of course, she's too young to remember exactly what happened. But I want her to be able to grow up to say, "I was there when my mother murdered Dixon." Imagine it—my little girl is going to grow up in a world where she'll never have to hear anybody say he's going to make something perfectly clear ever again! Or, "Let's make no mistake about it!" Or, "I'm a Quaker and that's why I hate war so much——" Never never never never. And I did it. I actually did it. I tell you, I still can't believe it. I drowned him. In cold water. *Me*.'

'And you, young man, let's move on to you. You're just walking up and down here outside the White House, very much as though you've lost something. You seem confused and bewildered. Can you tell us, in a few words, what it is you're searching for?'

'A cop. A policeman.'

'Why?'

'I want to turn myself in.'

'This is Brad Bathos, from the streets of Washington, where the mourners have come to gather, to pray, to weep, to lament and to hope. Back to Erect Severehead.'

'Erect, we're up here on top of the Washington Monument with the Chief of the Washington Police Force. Chief Shackles, how many people would you say are down there right now?'

'Oh, just around the monument alone we've got about twenty-five or thirty thousand; and I'd say there are twice that many over by the White House. And of course more are pouring in every hour.'

'Can you describe these people? Are they the usual sort of demonstrators you get here in Washington?'

'Oh no, no. These people don't want to disrupt anything. I would say they are actually bending over backwards to co-operate with the authorities. So far, at any rate.'

'What do you mean by so far?'

'Well, we haven't yet had to make any arrests. We're under orders from the White House *not* to arrest anyone under any conditions. As you can imagine, this is putting something of a strain on my men, particularly as just about everybody down here seems to have come for the purpose of *getting* himself arrested. I mean I've never seen anything like it. A lot of them are down on their knees begging to be taken in, and just about every Tom, Dick and Harry seems to have documents or photographs or fingerprints, proving that he is the one who killed the President. Of course, none of it is worth the paper it's written on. Some of it's kind of laughable, in fact, it's so unprofessional and obviously a slapdash last-minute job. But still and all, you got to give them credit for their fortitude. They grab hold of my men just like they had the goods on themselves, and actually try to handcuff themselves to the officer with their *own* handcuffs and get carted off to prison that way. We can't park a squad car anywhere, without half a dozen of them jumping into the back seat, and screaming, "Take me to J. Edgar Heehaw—and step on it." Now you can't arrest anybody without taking the proper procedural steps, but go try to explain that to a crowd like this. We're sort of humoring them, however, the best we can, and the ones who just won't quiet, we tell them to wait right where they are and we'll round them up later. What we're hoping for is a good thunderstorm during the night, that'll sort of break the back of the whole thing. Maybe if they stand around long enough in the rain they'll get the idea that nobody is going to arrest them no matter *how* much evidence they produce, and they'll go home.'

'But, Chief Shackles, suppose the rain doesn't come—suppose they are still jamming the streets in the morning. What about the workers trying to get to government offices——?'

'Well, they'll just have to suffer a little inconvenience, I'm afraid. Because I am not subjecting my men to the charge of false arrest just so somebody can get to his office in time for the morning coffee break. And then there are these orders from the White House.'

'Your assumption then is that all these people here are innocent, each and every one?'

'Absolutely. If they were guilty, they would be *resisting* arrest. They would be running away and so on. They would be screaming about their lawyers and their rights. I mean, that's how you can tell they're guilty in the first place. But all these people are saying is, "I did it, take me in." What sort of law enforcement officer is going to arrest a person for something like that?'

'This is Brad Bathos. Violence has erupted here on Pennsylvania Avenue, directly outside the White House gates where upwards of thirty thousand mourners have already gathered to bid farewell to a fallen leader. Even as Police Chief Shackles was praising this crowd for their obedience to authority and respect for the law, a free-for-all broke out among a group of fifteen men in business suits. Though police intervention was necessary, no arrests were made. I have here beside me one of the gentlemen who was involved in the violent episode, and by all appearances he is still rather upset. Sir, how did the violence begin?'

'Well, I was just standing here, minding my own business, trying to confess to an officer about murdering the President, when along comes this very fancy guy in a limousine and wearing a flower in his buttonhole, and he just steps in between me and the officers and he says *he* did it. And then the chauffeur gets out of the car and he starts pushing me back and saying let his boss do the talking, his boss really did it and he was a very busy man and so on and so forth and who did I think I was, acting so high and mighty. So then some colored guy comes up—and I don't have anything against colored guys, you know—but this one was real uppity and he starts saying we're both full of it, *he* did it, and the chauffeur tells him to get at the end of the line and wait his turn, and that really starts the thing going, and the next thing you know there are fifteen guys all swinging at one another, claiming *they* all did it, too. Well, if it wasn't for the officer, I'm not kidding, somebody might have gotten hurt. It could have been awful.'

'So you have nothing but praise for the police?'

'Well, yes—up to a point. I mean he broke this thing up one-two-three, but then when it was all over he *still* wouldn't make any arrests. In fact, once he'd separated us, he just disappeared, like the Lone Ranger used to. I can't find him anywhere. Some of the other guys want to find him, too. See, we gave him these confessions and all this incriminating evidence, and so on—and you know what he did with it? He just tore it up, even while he was running away. Fortunately, I had my secretary xerox all this stuff at my office, so I've got a copy at home, but a lot of these guys were foolish enough to give him the only copy of their confessions that they had. About the only *good* thing to come out of this is the possibility that because the fifteen of us were seen all huddled together on the pavement here, pounding each other's heads in, we might get picked up as a conspiracy. That is, if we can find a cop. But go try to find even a plainclothesman when you need one. Hey, you're not authorized to make an arrest, are you, by your network or something?'

'—and so in they continue to come. And now they have told us why. They come not as they came to Washington to mourn the death of President Charisma. Nor do they come as came they did to Atlanta, to follow behind the bier of the slain Martin Luther King. Nor come do they as to the railroad tracks they did, to wave farewell as the tragic train that bore the body of the murdered Robert Charisma carried to its final resting place, him. No, the crowd that cometh to Washington tonighteth, cometh not in innocence and bewilderment, like little children berefteth of a father. Rather, cometh they in guilt, cometh they to confesseth, cometh they to say, "I too am guilty," to the police and the FBI. It is a sight, moving and

121

profound, and furnishes evidence surely, if evidence there need surely be, of a nation that has cometh of age. For what is maturity, in men or in nations, but the willingness to bear the burden—and the dignity—of responsibility? And surely responsible it is, mature it is, when in its darkest hour, a nation can look deep within its troubled and anguished blah blah blah blah blah blah blah the guilt of all. Of course, those there are who will seek a scapegoat, as those there will always be, human nature being what it is instead of what it should be. Those there are who will self-righteously stand up and shout, "Not me, not me." For they are not guilty, they are never guilty. It is always the other guy who is guilty: Bundy and Kissinger, Bonnie and Clyde, Calley and Capone, Manson and McNamara—yes, the list is endless of those whom they would make responsible for their own crimes. And that is what makes this demonstration here in Washington of collective guilt so blah blah blah blah blah blah blah blah blah. The blah blah of the spirit and the blah blah blah blah blah blah for which our sons have died blah blah blah blah blah blah reason and dignity blah blah blah blah blah dignity and reason. No, blame not those who gather here in Washington to confess to the murder of the President. Rather, praise them for their courage, their blah blah blah, their blah and their blah blah blah, for blah blah blah blah as are you and I. We are all guilty. And only at the risk of blah blah blah blah blah blah blah blah blah blah forget. This is Erect Severehead from the nation's blah.'

'—the masochists, the mainliners, the minorities who think they are the majorities, the mashers, the masturbators, the mental cases, the misanthropes, the momma's boys, the much-ado-about-nothingites, the milquetoasts——'

'Gentlemen, because of the developing interest around the nation in the situation here in Washington, we have decided to move somewhat faster than we had originally planned, and to release to you tonight the x-ray of the other hip. We hope that by releasing the x-rays of *both* of the President's hips, the right virtually within a few hours of the left, we will be able to

122

restore some perspective as regards this whole situation.'

'You mean by that the assassination, Blurb?'

'I don't know if I want to use a highly inflammatory word like that at a time like this. It may not sell newspapers, but I'd just as soon, for the sake of accuracy, stick to "the situation." '

'In other words, you are now admitting that there is "a situation." '

'I don't think we ever denied that.'

'What about the funeral, Blurb?'

'Let's deal with the situation first, then we'll get to the funeral. Any other questions?'

'Where is the President's body right now?'

'Resting comfortably.'

'Comfortably *in* the baggie or *out* of the baggie?'

'Gentlemen, don't push me. He's resting comfortably. That's the important thing.'

'Will he be buried in the baggie, Blurb? One report is that the First Lady has decided that given his dedication to the rights of the unborn, burial in the baggie would be fitting and proper. Like King's body being pulled by a mule train.'

'Whatever the First Lady decides, I'm sure it'll be in good taste.'

'Blurb, what about Mr. What's-his-name? He's still back of the podium saying it didn't happen, that it's a pack of lies. Do you have any idea what he's talking about?'

'No comment.'

'Blurb, is it true that the oath of office has already been secretly administered to the Vice President between speaking engagements, and that he actually is the President at this very moment?'

'Why would we do a thing like that? Absolutely not.'

'Mr. President, can you tell us now why the oath of office was administered to you secretly between speaking engagements, so that actually you were the new President even while you went around claiming that the stories of President Dixon's assassination were lies perpetrated by the enemies of this country?'

123

'I think the answer to that is obvious enough, gentlemen. You cannot have a country without a President any more than you would want to have a cackle-dooper without a predipitous, or, likewise, a caloodian without a pre-pregoratory predention. Of course, the dreedles, the drishakis and the dripnaps would give their eyeteeth to have it otherwise, but the sworn swaggatelle of this sirigible, and the truncation of our truthfulness will not be trampled and torn, so long as I, as President, vent such vindictiveness as the avengers varp.'

'President What's-his-name, there is an admittedly ugly rumor to the effect that the reason you denied any knowledge of the President's assassination was because you were fearful that otherwise the finger of suspicion might be pointed at you. Do you have anything to say about that admittedly ugly rumor?'

'Yes, I have this to say and I propose to say it so that there is no doubt about my feelings on this matter later. If the creeps and the cowards that crucify the crelinion, crip after crip, and who furthermore—and we have proof of this—have crossbowed the cradalious ever since the first crackadoes crusaded in the cause of caliphony, if they think they can cajulate and castigate and get away with it, there will be such a cacophony of cabs, cassanings and crinoleum through the criss and cratch of this country, that the crypto-callistans and the quasi-clapperforms will quiver rather than coopt the crokes.'

'Sir, while we're on the subject of admittedly ugly rumors, can you comment on one that suggests that the reason you kept saying the President was alive when you knew he was dead, was because you were fearful that either a coup on the part of the Cabinet, or an armed revolt by the people, would have prevented you from taking office, had you announced openly your intention to do so? Were you frightened that they wouldn't let you be President because you weren't qualified?'

'Far from fear, what I felt was a filarious frostification at the far-reaching fistula into which fate had feductively fastinguished me.'

'Sir, will you comment on Mrs. Dixon's decision to bury the President in his baggie at Prissier? Were you consulted on this, and if so, does it mean that your administration will be as committed as was his to the rights of the unborn and the sanctity of human life and so on?'

'Well, of course, not just me, but zillions and zillions of our zircos, zaps of our zilpags and zikons of our zikenites——'

'So the blah blah blah blah of state has been passed. Blah blah blah blah blah blah blah has ended and the republic that blah blah blah blah reason blah blah blah blah. Heavy are our blah blah blah blah blah blah blah blah blah corridors blah blah blah that he loved. And the cherry blossoms. Blah blah blah blah blah. Blah blah blah blah. Blah blah blah blah blah lest we blah blah blah blah blah our civilization with it. We can ill afford that. Blah blah blah blah blah back to normal blah blah blah blah. Blah blah blah blah blah blah blah blah blah blah. Blah blah blah blah of America, from the humblest citizen to the blah blah blah blah. Blah blah 1776 blah blah? Blah. Blah blah 1812 blah blah blah? Blah blah. Blah blah 1904–1907? Blah! Blah blah blah blah blah blah blah reason and dignity. Blah blah blah blah reason. Blah blah blah blah blah dignity. Blah blah blah blah blah blah fulfillment of the Ameriblah blah blah blah blah blah. Blah blah blah one hundred years ago. Blah blah blah blah of Galilee. And yet those would surrender hope blah blah blah blah blah. Blah blah blah blah cherry blossoms. Blah blah blah blah blah blah blah blah blah blah before him. Blah blah blah the republic. Blah blah blah the people. Blah blah blah blah blah nation's capital.'

THE EULOGY OVER THE BAGGIE

(As Delivered Live on Nationwide TV by the Reverend Billy Cupcake)

Now today I want you to turn with me to page 853 in your dictionaries. Our eulogy is from the letter 'L,' the twelfth letter of the alphabet, and our word is the fifth down in the left-hand column, directly below the word 'leaden.' Our word is 'leader.' Now how does Noah Webster define 'leader'?

Well, Noah writes, 'A leader is one who or one that which leads.' One who or one that which leads. One *who* or *that which* leads.

Just the day before yesterday I read an article in a current magazine by one of the top philosophers of all time and he wrote, 'Leaders are one of man's top necessities.' And in a recent Gallup Poll we've been reading where more than ninety-eight percent of the people of America believe in leadership. I was in a European country last summer and one of the top young people there told me that the teenagers in his country want leadership more than anything else. President Lincoln—before he was killed—said the same thing. So did Newton—Sir Isaac Newton, the great scientist—when he was alive.

Now when Noah tells us that a leader is one *who* or one *that which* leads, he is telling us what 'leader' means in the *ordinary* sense of the word. But I wonder if he who lies here before us in this baggie was a leader in the *ordinary* sense. I don't think he was. And I'll tell you why. I talked to a psychiatrist friend of mine only this morning and he said, 'He was not an ordinary leader.' And one of my friends, a distinguished surgeon who does heart transplants at one of our great hospitals, wrote me a letter and said the same thing: 'He was not a leader in the ordinary sense of the word.'

Well, you say, what was he then, if he wasn't a leader in the ordinary sense? He—and I repeat that—*he* was a leader in the *extra*ordinary sense of that word.

Now what does that mean, the *extra*ordinary sense of that word? Fortunately, Noah defines 'extraordinary' for us, too. You will find the definition on page 428 in your dictionaries, in the right-hand column, six words down, directly beneath 'extraneous.' *Extra*ordinary, Noah tells us, means, 'beyond what is ordinary; out of the regular and established order.' *Beyond* what is ordinary. *Out* of the regular and established order.

Now what does *that* mean? I read only the week before last in an Australian newspaper that I get in my home a story about a fellow who made news down there—and why did he make news down there? Why do I know about him thousands and thousands of miles away? Because he was *extra*ordinary in some way or another. He was that rare thing among men. He was himself and no one else. Himself and no one else.

And what does Noah tell us about 'himself'? 'Himself,' Noah says, 'an emphatic form of him.' An *emphatic* form of him. Here then is what was so *extra*ordinary about the leader around whose baggie we are gathered today. He was emphatically *him*self and no one else.

You know. Let me repeat that. You know, I have been to funerals of ordinary leaders the world round, and I know you have too, by way of the miracle of television. We all know the wonderful things that are said on these sorrowful occasions. But I think I have only to repeat the fine words that are intoned over the graves of ordinary dead dignitaries for you to see how truly *extra*ordinary was our own dear departed President, in and of himself. In and of himself, which, you remember, Noah tells us is the *emphatic* form of him.

Now I don't mean to disparage the ordinary leaders of this great globe by this comparison. I read a letter only three weeks ago Thursday that a radical young person wrote to his girl friend disparaging and scoffing and laughing at the leaders of this world. Now he may laugh. They laughed at Jeremiah, you know. They laughed at Lot. They laughed at Amos. They laughed at the Apostles. In our own time they laughed at the Marx Brothers. They laughed at the Ritz Brothers. They laughed at the Three Stooges. Yet these people became our top entertainers and earned the love and affection of millions. There are always the laughers and the scoffers. You know there used to be a top tune in all the jukeboxes called 'I'm Laughing on the Outside, Crying on the Inside.' And I read an article in a news magazine only Sunday before last by one of our top psychologists which says that eighty-five percent— eighty-five percent!—of those who laugh on the outside cry on the inside because of their personal unhappiness.

I am not then trying to disparage the ordinary leaders of the world by this comparison. I want only to illustrate to you the extraordinary leadership of the man who walked among us for a brief while in a business suit, and now is gone. Only yesterday morning at ten A.M., I overheard a lady in an elevator of one of our top hotels, say to a young person, 'There has never been another like him in history, there will never be another like him again.'

Now. Let me repeat that. Now, when an ordinary leader dies—and I mean by 'ordinary' just what Noah does, on page 853, the last word down in column one: 'of the usual kind' or 'such as is commonly met with'—when an *ordinary* leader dies, there always seem to be words and phrases aplenty with which to bury him. However, *how ever*, when an *extra*ordinary leader dies, a man who was *him*self and no one else—what then do we say?

Let's try a scientific experiment. Now science doesn't hold all the answers and many of my scientific friends tell me that all the time. Scie e, for instance, doesn't know what life is yet, and in a recent Gallup Poll did you know that five percent more Americans believe in life after death now than they did some twenty years ago? So science doesn't have all the answers, but it has provided us with many wonderful breakthroughs.

Let's try this scientific experiment. Let's try the phrases for an *ordinary* man on this *extra*ordinary man. And you tell me if you don't agree that as applies to him who lies here in his baggie, they are hollow to the ear and false to the heart, and vice versa. Let's see if when this experiment is over, you don't say to me, 'Why, Billy, you're right, they don't describe him at all. They describe one *who* or one *that which* leads, but not him who was emphatically *him*self and no other.'

I'm going to ask that we bow our heads now. Every head bowed and every eye closed, and listen.

They say of an *ordinary* leader, when and if he dies, of course—he was a man of broad outlook;

Or, he was a man of great passion;

Or, he was a man of deep conviction;

Or, he was a defender of human rights;

Or, he was a soldier of humanity;

128

Or, he was scholarly, eloquent and wise;

Or, he was a simple, peace-loving man, brave and kind;

Or, he was a man who embodied the ideals of his people;

Or, he was a man who fired the imagination of a generation.

They say of an *ordinary* man, when and if he dies, that the loss is incalculable to the nation and the world.

They say of an *ordinary* man, when and if he dies, that all will be better for his having passed their way.

Need I go any further? There was an article in a current magazine last month by a professor who is an authority on human behavior, and he writes that you can tell when a crowd of people is in agreement with you. Well, the professor is correct. Because I know that you are all saying to yourselves, 'Why, Billy, you're right—in vain do I listen for the words or word that describes he who lies here in this baggie; for these are phrases that summon up the image of an ordinary leader, not the *extra*ordinary leader we have lost.'

What word or words then will describe this *extra*ordinary man? I was in an African country one year ago this July and I heard a top political expert there call him 'The President of the United States.' The President of the United States. In another African country I heard about a teenage girl who called him 'The Leader of the Free World.' The Leader of the Free World. And a lawyer friend of mine, a well-known judge, who lives in South America wrote me a letter not too long ago and he had an interesting thing to say. He said he heard a man in an elevator in a top hotel in Buenos Aires, Argentina, call him 'Commander-in-Chief of the American Armed Forces.' Commander-in-Chief of the Armed Forces.

Yet are these the words in which he lived in the hearts of his fellow countrymen? Perhaps that is what he was to the rest of the world. But to we who knew him, nothing so majestic or formal could begin to communicate the kind of man he was and the esteem in which he was held. Because to us he was not a leader in the *ordinary* sense—he was a leader in the *extra*ordinary sense. And that is why we who knew him think of him by a name as unpretentious and unceremonious as the name you might give to your own pet, a name as homey and familiar as you might bestow upon a little puppy.

I'm going to ask that we bow our heads again. Every head bowed and every eye closed, while we all share in the remembrance of the name by which he was known to we who knew him best, the name by which we called him in our hearts, even if we were too shy or too timid to speak it with our lips while he walked among us in a business suit. And how appropriate that it is a name even a puppy could bear, for we all remember as much as anything about him, the deep reverence he had for dogs.

The name was a simple one, my friends. The name was Tricky. Yes, to you, to me, and to all Americans for generations to come, Tricky he was and Tricky he shall be.

And now, all heads bowed and every eye closed, let us pray. Oh God, who alone art ever merciful in sparing of punishment, humbly we pray Thee on behalf of Thy servant, a man called Tricky...

SIX

ON THE COMEBACK TRAIL;
OR, TRICKY IN HELL

My fellow Fallen:

Let me say at the outset that I of course agree with much of what Satan has said here tonight in his opening statement. I know that Satan feels as deeply as I do about what has to be done to make Wickedness all that it can and should be in the creation. For let there be no mistake about it: we are engaged in a deadly competition with the Kingdom of Righteousness. There isn't any question in my mind but that the God of Peace is out, as He Himself has said, 'to crush' us 'under His feet,' and that He and His gang of angels will stop at nothing to accomplish this end. I could not agree more with Satan when he says that our goal is not just to keep Wickedness for ourselves, but to extend it to all creation, because that is Hell's destiny. To extend it to all creation because the aim of the Righteous is not just to hold their own, but to extend Righteousness. But we cannot be victorious over Righteousness with a strategy of simply holding the line. My disagreement with Satan then is not about the goals for Hell, but about the means to reach those goals.

Now Satan has said that we are ahead in this competition with Righteousness. I cannot agree with that appraisal of the situation. As I look at Hell today, I believe that we are following programs of an outdated leadership. I believe we are following programs many of which have not worked in the past and will not work in the future. I say that the programs and leadership that have failed under Satan's administration are not the programs and the leadership that Hell needs now. I say that the damned and the doomed do not want to go back to the policies of the Garden of Eden. I say that the Sons and Daughters of Disobedience deserve a Devil of consummate depravity, a Devil who will devote himself not to old and worn-out iniquities, but to bold new programs in Evil that will overturn God's kingdom and plunge men into eternal death. What we need down here is not just high hopes. What we need is crafty wiles and untiring zeal. In the field of executive leadership, I believe it is essential that the Devil not only set the tone, but he also must lead; he must act as he talks.

Frankly, I don't think this is the kind of leadership we have been getting. Now since my arrival I have traveled to the very edges of the outer darkness. I have been down to the bottom of the bottomless pit. I have been burned in the unquenchable fire and have joined you in the comfortless gloom. I have talked to sinners from all walks of life. I have eaten with degenerates and blasphemed with the impious. I have looked into the eyes of the depraved and the malicious. I have familiarized myself with viciousness and baseness of all kinds. And one thing I have noted as I have traveled from one end of Hell to the other is the wonderful belief our people have in Wickedness. I tell you, with great pride, that I have never seen anything to equal our corruption. And that is why I don't think we have to settle for second best. I don't think we have to settle for anything less than a Devil who is the very embodiment of malice. And I humbly submit to you, the denizens of the greatest infernal region in all creation, that if elected, I would be that kind of Devil.

I was fortunate enough to hear an awful lot of weeping and gnashing of teeth on my trip around Hell, and I think the strongest impression I came away with was this: that you lost souls out there are just as sick and tired as I am of hearing the Devil downgraded and Hell itself dismissed as 'old-fashioned' and 'out-of-date.' Well, maybe it is 'old-fashioned' in some circles, but to those of us who live here, Hell happens to be home. And dating back as it does to the beginning of time, it happens to have been home to some of the most illustrious names in history. And I think that with that kind of history and that kind of record, it is high time we put Hell back on the map, and high time the Devil was given his due.

Now I can only say, in this regard, that maybe Satan is satisfied with the fact that at least one half of the people presently on earth—and I know this, because I just came from there—at least one half of those people no longer believe in the existence of Hell, let alone its influence in world affairs. And maybe Satan is satisfied that the Devil, the highest official in the underworld, once the very symbol of nefariousness to millions, is considered in the upper regions to have absolutely no power at all over the decisions made there by men. And maybe Satan is satisfied when at least two thirds of the children in the world go to bed at night without any fear of fire or brimstone, or an undying worm gnawing at the heart. Incidentally, in that connection, they don't even fear the pitchfork. And maybe that's all right with Satan, too. However, let me make my position very clear. It's not all right with me. Maybe Satan is satisfied with the status quo; well, I'm not. I say that when Hell is nothing more than a dirty word in the mouths of most people living today, then something is wrong, and something has to be done about it.

What has happened to 'the Devil's net' we used to hear so much about? My fellow Fallen, it is full of holes.

What has happened to 'the power of the Devil' that used to terrify the hearts of men? My fellow Fallen, it has run out of steam.

And when was the last time you heard the phrase 'the work of Satan'? Can you even remember? Maybe that's because after all these millennia in office, Satan is satisfied with the status quo.

But I'm not. I say the Devil's work is never done. I say he has a responsibility to get up there among the living and wage war against the forces of Righteousness. I say he has a responsibility to the denizens of Hell, and to all souls everywhere who aspire to Wickedness, to oppose truth with falsehood. I say he has a responsibility to obscure light with darkness. I say he has a responsibility to entangle men's minds in error. I say he has a responsibility to stir up hatred. I say he has a responsibility to kindle contentions and combats. And I say any Devil who does less than this is not deserving of the title 'Prince of Darkness,' and does serious harm to the power and prestige of Hell and to the security of the Wicked everywhere.

Now you may answer, 'That is all fine and dandy, Mr. President, but what qualifications do you bring with you to the job of being a responsible Devil?'

I know as well as you do the claims my opponent makes for his experience in office. I know what has been written in grudging tribute of him, by no less than our own adversaries in Heaven. 'When Satan lies,' they say, 'he speaks according to his own nature, for he is a liar and the father of lies.' And let there be no mistake about my position on this issue: I have the highest regard for his long and distinguished record as a liar. I know that I, like so many of you out there in the fires and down there in the pit, owe a deep debt of gratitude to the example of his never-say-die spirit, where lying is concerned.

To interject a personal note, you know I was born an opportunist, out in California, and during my years in public life I had the privilege of wheeling and dealing with other opportunists as well. And I think I speak for all opportunists when I say that Satan has been a constant source of inspiration to us from time immemorial, in good times and in bad. Surely I would want it understood throughout this campaign, that I respect not only the tenacity with which he lies, but his sincerity in lying. And of course I would hope that he would agree that I am just as sincere in my lying as he is in his.

But let me make one thing perfectly clear. Much as I respect and admire his lies, I don't think that lies are something to stand on. I think they are something to build on. I don't think anyone, man or demon, can ever rely upon the lies he has told in the past, bold and audacious as they may have been at the time, to distort today's realities. We live in an era of rapid and dramatic change. My own experience has shown that yesterday's lies are just not going to confuse today's problems. You cannot expect to mislead people next year the way you misled them a year ago, let alone a million years ago. And that is why, with all due respect to my opponent's

134

experience, I say we need a new administration in Hell, an administration with new horns, new half-truths, new horrors and new hypocrisies. I say we need a new commitment to Evil, new strategems and contrivances to make our dream of a totally fallen world a reality.

And now let me say a word to those who point to my own record as President of the United States and contend that it is less than it could have been, as regards suffering and anguish for all of the people, regardless of race, creed or color. Let me remind these critics that I happen to have held that high office for less than one term before I was assassinated. Now not even Satan, I think, with the support of all his legions, would claim that he could bring a nation with a strong democratic tradition and the highest standard of living in the world to utter ruination in only a thousand days. Indeed, despite my brief tenure in the 'White' House, I firmly believe that I was able to maintain and perpetuate all that was evil in American life when I came to power. Furthermore I think I can safely say that I was able to lay the groundwork for new oppressions and injustices and to sow seeds of bitterness and hatred between the races, the generations and the social classes that hopefully will plague the American people for years to come. Surely I did nothing whatsoever to decrease the eventuality of a nuclear holocaust, but rather continued to make progress in that direction by maintaining policies of belligerence, aggression and subversion around the globe. I think I might point with particular pride to Southeast Asia, where I was able to achieve considerable growth in just the sort of human misery that the vengeful and vindictive souls here in our great inferno would wish upon the whole of mankind.

Now of course I do not claim sole responsibility for the devastation and misery visited by my country upon the Vietnamese, the Laotians and the Cambodians. In fact, I know that in the years to come you are going to have the privilege of meeting many of the men who were equally as devoted as was I, and who worked long hard hours with great dedication and self-sacrifice, as did I, to make life a nightmare in that region for those Asian human beings. I know when they get here they are going to make a great contribution to Hell, and let me say in that connection that if I am elected Devil, I will not hesitate to avail myself of their counsel and advice here, as I did there.

While it is true then that I was not the sole author, leader and architect of this great program for suffering launched by my country in Southeast Asia, I will say this: when the opportunity to take charge of our program was presented to me, I did not stand pat on the butchery and carnage of my predecessors. Because I know, as do you, that where slaughter is concerned we cannot stand pat. We cannot stand pat for the reason that we're in a race, as I've indicated. We can't stand pat because it is essential with the conflict that we have around the globe that we not just hold our own, that we not just keep suffering for ourselves, but that we extend it to every last man, woman and child. And I am confident that if you will look at the record, you will see that this is just what I was able to accomplish throughout Southeast Asia. I think you will agree that in the very brief time allotted to me I managed to seize upon the opportunity provided me by my predecessors and, with the aid of the United States Air Force, I turned that part of the globe into nothing less than Hell on earth.

Now I realize, as you do, that despite my record in Southeast Asia, there are still those who would impugn my reputation by pointing to certain so-called 'humane' or 'benevolent' actions that I undertook while President of the United States. Well, let me say, as regards these wholly unfounded attacks upon my bad name, that I intend, after this broadcast, to issue a black paper, showing that in every single instance where they claim I was 'humane' or 'benevolent,' I was in actual fact motivated solely by political self-interest, and acted with utter indifference, if not outright contempt and cynicism, for the welfare of anybody other than myself. If and when any good whatsoever accrued to anything but me and my career, it was—as I am confident the black paper will make perfectly clear—wholly unintentional and inadvertent.

Now I am not saying that ignorance of benign consequences

is any excuse for a demon who aspires to be your Devil. I am only admitting to you that I was not so hideous on earth as I might have been. But then I am sure that the great majority of demons in Hell weren't either, and that you share with me regrets about wasted opportunities and pangs of conscience. But let there be no mistake about it: I am no longer a man burdened by all the limitations and weaknesses of that condition, such as conscience, caution and consideration for one's reputation. And I am no longer the President of the United States, with all the barriers and obstructions that stand between the holder of that powerful office and his own capacity for evil. I am at long last a citizen of Hell, and let me tell you, that is a great challenge and a great opportunity. And that is why I can assure you, my fellow Fallen, that down here where no holds are barred and nothing is sacred, you are going to see a New Dixon, a Dixon such as I could only dream of being while still an American human being, a Dixon who humbly submits that he has what it takes in experience and energy to be the kind of Devil all you lost souls deserve.

Now in order that the four demons on tonight's panel can proceed to questioning Satan and myself—and let me say, I welcome their questions—I shall now bring my opening statement to a close. But before I do, I want to make one last thing particularly clear to the denizens of Hell, and that is this. In terms of eternity, I am a relative newcomer to the Realm of Wickedness. But I am a student of history also, and I must say that in reading through the record of the current administration, and in particular its relations with the Kingdom of Righteousness, I have been shocked by a blatant example of what I can only call an attitude of appeasement—an attitude, I am sorry to say, of outright submission and surrender. I am talking, of course, of the famous Job case.

Now I know that in defense of his actions in that case Satan has described to you in great detail all the sufferings that he heaped upon this good man, Job. And I am not going to say to you that he did not torment him in the extreme. I am not going to try to build myself up by downgrading the job he did

137

on Job's sheep and his servants, and the loathsome sores with which he afflicted him from head to foot. There is no question but that the program of pain and punishment devised by Satan was the right one in those circumstances.

Yet the question still remains, thousands of years after the event, under whose auspices and in whose behalf was that program devised? Under the auspices of Hell? In behalf of the cause of Wickedness?

My fellow Fallen, the answer is no. I am afraid that if you read the record, as I have done, you will find that it was under the auspices of Heaven, and in behalf of Righteousness, that your own Devil planned and executed Job's program of P&P, a program by the way involving a considerable expenditure of our resources. I am afraid that if you read the record you will find your own Devil taking his orders from none other than the Lord God Himself. I am afraid you will find that your own Devil did not so much as undertake one Evil act without first obtaining the permission of God. I am afraid that you will find that the reason he exercised the patience of Job was not to drive him from obedience and destroy him, but to serve God's justice—and, what is worse, to cause God's righteousness to shine forth.

Now Satan has indicated on several occasions during this campaign that I have been misrepresenting his role in the Job case. In order to set the record straight once and for all, I am going to use my remaining few minutes to read to you verbatim from the minutes of the meeting that took place between God and Satan at that time. And I leave it to you, the degenerate and the debauched, the dissolute and the depraved, to judge whether the charges I have made during the campaign, and that I repeat here tonight on this broadcast, constitute 'a reckless distortion and deliberate misreading of history.' I leave it to you to judge whether Satan was, as he claims, working 'diabolically' and 'fiendishly' for the cause of Wickedness, or whether he was, to put it in language everyone can understand, acting in accordance with Divine Will.

This document I am holding in my claw is called the Holy Scripture. It doesn't lie. That is why it is nothing less than the

138

Bible of our enemies. This is their number-one best seller of all time. This is the book with which they brainwash their children. Contained here are all the truths with which they intend to conquer the world. You can open it anywhere and find enough wisdom and beauty on a single page to disgust and outrage every loyal and hard-working citizen of Hell.

Let me read to you from the secret conversation between God and Satan, as documented in their Bible:

THE LORD: *Whence have you come?*

SATAN: *From going to and fro on the earth, and from walking up and down on it.*

THE LORD: *Have you considered my servant Job, that there is none like him on the earth, a blameless and upright man, who fears God and turns away from evil?*

SATAN: *Does Job fear God for naught? Hast thou not put a hedge about him and his house and all that he has, on every side? Thou has blessed the work of his hands, and his possessions have increased in the land. But* [and I am still quoting here from Satan], *but put forth thy hand now, and touch all that he has, and he will curse thee to thy face.*

THE LORD: *Behold, all that he has is in your power, only upon himself do not put forth your hand.*

That was the instruction given Satan by the Lord. And what did Satan do? Exactly as God told him to. Yes, my fellow Fallen, your own Devil became an instrument of God's wrath.

Let me read to you now from the minutes of the second secret meeting that took place in an unspecified location between the Emperor of Wickedness and the God of Peace. For the sake of brevity I will read to you only the most pertinent material.

THE LORD (*speaking of Job*): *He still holds fast to his integrity.*

SATAN: *... Put forth thy hand now, and touch his bone and his flesh, and he will curse thee to thy face.*

THE LORD: *Behold, he is in your power; only spare his life.*

And having received this second set of instructions, what

did Satan do? Let me read it to you, just as it is written here in their Bible. 'So Satan went forth from the presence of the Lord, and afflicted Job with loathsome sores from the sole of his foot to the crown of his head.'

And did Satan spare Job's life, as God instructed him to? I am afraid the answer is yes, he did that too.

We all remember, I am sure, the unhappy ending to that story. Job's faith was not broken; it was strengthened and increased. And the Lord, as the record here states, 'gave Job twice as much as he had before.'

(Tricky closes Bible. Quickly wipes perspiration from his scales with the back of his claw)

My fellow Fallen, I challenge Satan to refute these charges that I have made here tonight. I challenge Satan to deny his role in the Job case. I challenge him to deny that he acted willingly and knowingly in behalf of the sworn enemies of Hell. I challenge him to deny that if this was not an outright act of treason, it was one so neglectful of the security interests of the Wicked, that Satan might just as well have been in the employ of the Righteous.

Now Satan may prefer to call these actions of his 'fiendish' and 'diabolical.' But I call what he has done here surrender, and let me tell you something—I think that's what the leaders in Heaven are calling it, too. Because make no mistake about it—I know the other side. I have met with their representatives. I know the kind of ruthless and fanatical people they are, and I can assure you, if you surrender to their Will, if you think it will stop them to surrender a single soul to their Righteousness, you are sadly mistaken. That will only whet their appetite for more. Because this God of Peace does not just want Job. He wants all the Jobs. And if we do not stop him each and every time, the day will come, my friends, when he will be hammering here at the Gates of Hell.

And that is why I say the time has come to stop appeasing the God of Peace. That is why I say the time has come to step up our own activities, and launch a new offensive in this battle for the minds and hearts and souls of men. For it is nothing less than an ideological battle that we are fighting; and that is why we need a Devil who is willing and able to stand on his ideals. It isn't the size or the age of a man's horns that counts—it's what he's going to do with them. It's our whole lives that you should be judging here tonight. It's what we stand for. It's what we believe. What I am trying to indicate to you tonight is that the tide of history is on our side, and that we can keep it on our side, because we're on the right side, and that's the side of Evil. And let there be no mistake about it: if I am elected Devil, I intend to see Evil triumph in the end; I intend to see that our children, and our children's children, need never know the terrible scourge of Righteousness and Peace.

Thank you.

THEN I SAW AN ANGEL COMING DOWN FROM HEAVEN, HOLDING IN HIS HAND THE KEY OF THE BOTTOMLESS PIT AND A GREAT CHAIN. AND HE SEIZED THE DRAGON, THAT ANCIENT SERPENT, WHO IS THE DEVIL ... AND BOUND HIM FOR A THOUSAND YEARS, AND THREW HIM INTO THE PIT, AND SHUT IT AND SEALED IT OVER HIM, THAT HE SHOULD DECEIVE THE NATIONS NO MORE ...

THE BOOK OF REVELATION

A SELECTION OF FINE READING AVAILABLE IN CORGI BOOKS

Novels

☐ 552 08651 7	THE HAND-REARED BOY	*Brian W. Aldiss*	25p
☐ 552 07938 3	THE NAKED LUNCH	*William Burroughs*	37½p
☐ 552 08849 8	THE GLASS VIRGIN	*Catherine Cookson*	40p
☐ 552 08913 3	ROONEY	*Catherine Cookson*	25p
☐ 552 08793 9	THE PRETTY BOYS	*Simon Cooper*	35p
☐ 552 08440 9	THE ANDROMEDA STRAIN	*Michael Crichton*	35p
☐ 552 08868 4	I KNEW DAISY SMUTEN	ed. *Hunter Davies*	40p
☐ 552 08851 X	CHEAP DAY RETURN	*R. F. Delderfield*	35p
☐ 552 08934 6	THE INTERNS	*Richard Frede*	35p
☐ 552 08912 5	SUCH GOOD FRIENDS	*Lois Gould*	40p
☐ 552 08915 X	HIJACKED	*David Harper*	35p
☐ 552 08125 6	CATCH-22	*Joseph Heller*	35p
☐ 552 08652 5	THY DAUGHTER'S NAKEDNESS	*Myron S. Kauffmann*	62½p
☐ 552 08932 X	ALSO THE HILLS	*Frances Parkinson Keyes*	45p
☐ 552 08833 1	HOW FAR TO BETHLEHEM?	*Norah Lofts*	35p
☐ 552 08888 9	REQUIEM FOR IDOLS	*Norah Lofts*	25p
☐ 552 08933 8	THE TERRACOTTA PALACE	*Anne Maybury*	35p
☐ 552 08791 2	HAWAII	*James A. Michener*	75p
☐ 552 08867 6	THE COLLECTION	*Paulo Montano*	40p
☐ 552 08916 8	ROXANA AND ALEXANDER	*Helga Moray*	30p
☐ 552 08124 8	LOLITA	*Vladimir Nabokov*	35p
☐ 552 08630 4	PRETTY MAIDS ALL IN A ROW	*Francis Pollini*	40p
☐ 552 07954 5	RUN FOR THE TREES	*James S. Rand*	35p
☐ 552 08887 0	VIVA RAMIREZ!	*James S. Rand*	40p
☐ 552 08930 3	STORY OF O	*Pauline Reage*	50p
☐ 552 08597 9	PORTNOY'S COMPLAINT	*Philip Roth*	40p
☐ 552 08814 5	SOMETHING OF VALUE	*Robert Ruark*	40p
☐ 552 08945 1	THE HONEY BADGER	*Robert Ruark*	55p
☐ 552 08852 8	SCANDAL'S CHILD	*Edmund Schiddel*	40p
☐ 552 08372 0	LAST EXIT TO BROOKLYN	*Hubert Selby Jr.*	50p
☐ 552 08931 1	ZARA	*Joyce Stranger*	30p
☐ 552 07807 7	VALLEY OF THE DOLLS	*Jacqueline Susann*	40p
☐ 552 08523 5	THE LOVE MACHINE	*Jacqueline Susann*	40p
☐ 552 08091 8	TOPAZ	*Leon Uris*	40p
☐ 552 08384 4	EXODUS	*Leon Uris*	40p
☐ 552 08481 6	FOREVER AMBER Vol. 1	*Kathleen Winsor*	35p
☐ 552 08482 4	FOREVER AMBER Vol. 2	*Kathleen Winsor*	35p

War

☐ 552 08935 4	ACCIDENTAL AGENT (illustrated)	*John Goldsmith*	35p
☐ 552 08874 9	SS GENERAL	*Sven Hassel*	35p
☐ 552 08779 3	ASSIGNMENT: GESTAPO	*Sven Hassel*	35p
☐ 552 08855 2	THE WILLING FLESH	*Willi Heinrich*	35p
☐ 552 08873 0	THE DOOMSDAY SQUAD	*Clark Howard*	25p
☐ 552 08920 6	SECURITY RISK	*Gilbert Hackforth-Jones*	25p
☐ 552 08892 7	THE FORTRESS	*Raleigh Trevelyan*	30p
☐ 552 08936 2	JOHNNY GOT HIS GUN	*Dalton Trumbo*	30p
☐ 552 08893 5	THE ENEMY	*Wirt Williams*	30p
☐ 552 08798 X	VIMY! (illustrated)	*Herbert Fairlie Wood*	30p
☐ 552 08919 2	JOHNNY PURPLE	*John Wyllie*	25p

Romance

☐ 552 08878 1	NURSE IN THE SUN	*Sheila Brandon*	25p
☐ 552 08941 9	THE BEDSIDE MANNER	*Kate Norway*	25p
☐ 552 08924 9	CASUALTY SPEAKING	*Kate Norway*	25p
☐ 552 08897 8	IF YOU SPEAK LOVE	*Jean Ure*	25p

Science Fiction

☐ 552 08925 7	THE BEST FROM NEW WRITINGS IN S.F.	ed. *John Carnell*	25p
☐ 552 08942 7	A WILDERNESS OF STARS	ed. *William Nolan*	30p
☐ 552 08804 8	THE AGE OF THE PUSSYFOOT	*Frederik Pohl*	25p
☐ 552 08860 9	VENUS PLUS X	*Theodore Sturgeon*	25p

General

All these books are available at your bookshop or newsagent: or can be ordered direct from the publisher. Just tick the titles you want and fill in the form below.

CORGI BOOKS, Cash Sales Department. P. O. Box, Falmouth, Cornwall.
Please send cheque or postal order. No currency, and allow 5p per book to cover the cost of postage and packing in the U.K., and overseas.

NAME ....

ADDRESS ....

(APRIL 72) ....